CRISPIN

AT THE EDGE OF THE WORLD

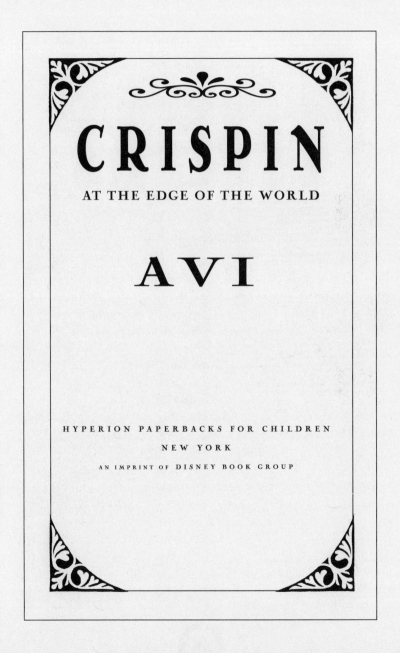

CRISPIN

AT THE EDGE OF THE WORLD

AVI

HYPERION PAPERBACKS FOR CHILDREN

NEW YORK

AN IMPRINT OF DISNEY BOOK GROUP

First Hyperion Paperbacks edition, 2008
3 5 7 9 10 8 6 4
Library of Congress Cataloging-in-Publication Data on file.
ISBN-13: 978-1-4231-0305-9
ISBN-10: 1-4231-0305-X
V475-2873-0   12212
Go to www.hyperionbooksforchildren.com to download
the discussion guide and author interview for
Crispin: At the Edge of the World.

For Anne Dunn

ENGLAND, A.D. 1377

The more I came to know of the world,
the more I knew I knew it not.

1

T WAS A JUNE MORNING when Bear and I passed beyond Great Wexly's walls and left the crowded and treacherous city behind. The June sun was warm, the sky above as blue as my Blessed Lady's spotless robe; our triumphant sense of liberty kept me giddy with joy. Hardly able to contain myself, I more than once cried out, "My name is Crispin!" for all the world to hear.

I carried Bear's sack, which contained little more than his music-making recorder and his fire-making tools, plus the few pennies we had eked out with our music and dance. His juggler's double-pointed hat, replete with bells, was the glorious crown that capped my head.

At first we sang, played music, and stepped lightly while

thanking Jesus profusely for our deliverance. What more, I thought, could my newly found soul require?

Yet though our spirits were as high as any cloud-leaping lark, it became increasingly clear that while the dungeon from which I'd freed Bear had not broken his soul, it had greatly reduced his strength. Indeed, as the day waxed he seemed to wane. More and more he leaned on me. Unshod feet had him limping. Though it was summer, his garment—no more than an old wool cloak—left him in need of warmth.

By midmorning, when our exuberance had all but ebbed, I said, "Bear, I think we need to find a place for you to rest and eat. And some decent clothing."

"Easier to say," he replied, "than do."

I held up our sack. "Bear," I said, "we have the quarter-penny to spare."

He shook his great, red-bearded head. "Crispin, we can't rest. Not yet."

"Bear, we've won our liberty."

"I'm afraid," he growled, "the most lethal of all sleep potions is success."

"What does *that* mean?"

"We've escaped. But don't doubt it, we'll be pursued. I'm as easy to find as a cardinal in a flock of ravens. And there are many now who would like to catch me." Bear had been a spy for John Ball's secret and illegal brotherhood, which sought to regain people's ancient liberties. It meant he had many enemies.

I did too—for different reasons.

Bear's words so reined in my good spirits that I looked about with apprehension. We were traveling on a deep-rutted, muddy track that ran as straight as any arrow. "Made by Caesar's great legions," Bear had told me. To one side lay thick forest. The other side was open, hilly land. Bear's warning made me wonder if those who wished us harm might crest the horizon at any time.

True, we had passed many a plodding peasant and foot-sore pilgrim, with scallop badge over heart and staff in hand. There had been fat merchants aplenty too, on thin horses, likely heading to the fair at Great Wexly. Though I had spied no one who alarmed me, quite naturally, they had gazed upon Bear. For God had made Bear a huge fellow with massive arms and legs and a great belly before all. His bald head was equally striking to behold, with great red beard, fuzzy eyebrows of the same hue, large nose and mouth, if small eyes. To see Bear was to know why he bore the name of beast—and yet, most surely he was a man, and one not likely to go unnoticed.

We had come upon some scattered houses, cottages, huts, and even an old, abandoned church. Perhaps a village had been there, but time or sickness had turned it to all but naught.

As I looked about, I spied a house from which a broom hung. I recognized it as an alestake: those within had brewed more ale than they could keep and the broom was set out as a signal to tempt passersby to purchase. My hope was that there would be bread as well.

"Bear," I said, pointing to the alestake, "look! The food and drink should be cheap. It will do you good."

"We're still too near Great Wexly," he cautioned.

"It will take only moments," I coaxed.

Bear considered, and then said, "As you wish,"—words, no doubt, called forth by his exhaustion. So it was we turned our steps off the road.

The house was large, a half-timbered structure with a few small and shuttered windows, its roof thick-thatched. Noting the tilled fields just behind, I supposed a free yeoman dwelled within. In the foreyard, geese strutted, clucking and hissing at one another. An old wooden trestle table had been set out, along with benches suggesting the dwellers offered food with some regularity. Just the thought made my stomach speak with hunger.

Upon reaching the house, Bear dropped heavily on a bench set to one side of the door. Right off, he shut his eyes and set his face toward the warming sun. It was, I realized, the first time since he'd been arrested in the city that he had been at ease.

Glad of it, I went to the split front door and rapped upon it.

In answer to my summons, the top part of the door opened a crack. A dark eye peered out. I must have been judged no threat, for the next moment the door swung wide.

The man who revealed himself was a broad-shouldered, powerfully built fellow of middling age, with long, ill-sheared black hair. A few days' growth of beard made his scowling mouth appear grim. Over his kirtle he wore the leather vest of an archer. The first and second fingers of his right hand were extra muscled and callused from— I assumed—pulling a bowstring to his ear. He looked vaguely familiar, but I was unable to claim him in my memory.

"Good morrow to you, boy," he said, although his voice carried little welcome. Moreover, he frowned so that his brow became as beetled as a well-plowed field.

"And to you, sir," I returned. "If it pleases, I saw your alestake. I'd like to purchase bread and drink."

"Have you anything to pay?" the man asked. His eyes squinted as if to take my measure, or his aim.

"Enough," I replied, "for me and my foot-weary master."

"What master?" he demanded.

I gestured. "He sits right here, sir."

Not bothering to look, the man muttered something that sounded like a curse as he withdrew into the darkness of his house.

How good it was to rest. Bear remained on his bench, eyes closed, face turned to the sun's kind heat. I took myself to the table where I sat, head in my arms. As I had not slept for two days, a surge of weariness swept through me.

The man returned, kicking open the lower door with a *thud* loud enough to make me sit up. Only then did I note the sheathed dagger that hung upon his hip. Not that I cared: he was carrying two wooden mazers full of drink, and barley bread was tucked under his arm.

My mouth watered.

The man set the mazers down and dropped the bread. "Where's your master?" he demanded.

"Right there," I said, nodding toward Bear.

The man turned round—and started. "By the wounds of Christ!" he cried when he saw Bear. "It's you!"

2

IS CRY STARTLED ME, and made Bear blink open his eyes. "We thought you dead," said the man to Bear. It was as much an accusation as a statement.

"All in God's good time," returned Bear, scrutinizing the man with his red-rimmed eyes. "How do you know me?" he asked. "And who is *we?*"

Instead of answering, the man swung about to look at me as if to reassess who *I* was. I recalled him then. He was a member of John Ball's rebel brotherhood, which had met at a shoemaker's shop in Great Wexly. At that meeting, Bear had helped this man and others to escape, though it resulted in his being taken prisoner.

The man turned back to Bear and asked, "Aren't you the one they call Bear?

"I am."

"The spy," the man said, not kindly. "How did you free yourself?"

Bear considered the question and then said, "The boy freed me."

"Lord Furnival's bastard?"

Bear frowned. "His name is Crispin."

"This one?" the man demanded, turning back to me.

"Himself."

Alarmed, I rose to my feet, though I did not know what to do. It was hardly the moment to tell him that to ransom Bear's liberty, I'd renounced any claim to my noble name.

The man considered me with harsh contempt before turning back to Bear. "Why have you come here?"

"Be assured," said Bear, holding up one of his large hands as if to show it empty, "it's by chance. We're trying to get as far from Great Wexly as we can. Passing by, the boy saw your broom. We're weary. Hungry. I'd no idea you lived here. In faith, I don't even know your name."

"Have you abandoned the brotherhood?"

Bear paused. "My friend," he said, "the only thing I wish to abandon is my fatigue."

"We're all weary," snapped the man. "Did you give names in exchange for your freedom?"

"Not I," said Bear.

"Watt the butcher has been taken. So too, Guy, the miller's man. We don't know what's become of them."

"God bring them quick release," said Bear, making the

sign of the cross. "I'm from other parts. By Saint Peter, I don't know any of your names."

The man glanced about, as if others might be lurking near. Momentarily, he fixed his eyes on me.

I was so agitated I hardly knew where to look.

"Then was it this boy," he persisted, "who bought your freedom with our names?"

Bear sighed. "The sole payment he gave was his courage."

"I don't believe you," said the man.

"That's as you may," said Bear. "But, as Our Sacred Lady is witness, what I say is true."

I kept wishing Bear would *do* something. I just wanted to leave.

"Then explain if you will," cried the man, growing more raddled each moment, "why among those held only you are free?"

"I cannot," said Bear.

"The authorities would never let you go without something in exchange."

"I know nothing about our brothers," said Bear. "I saw no one else where I was held. God knows they pressed me, but you may be sure I gave them nothing. I wouldn't do so to save my soul."

"I don't believe it."

Bear snorted with contempt. "Believe what you wish."

"I say you're an informer!" cried the man. "A traitor to the brotherhood!" He turned then, and with a broad stroke of his hand and arm, swept bowls and bread away, sending all aground. "I'll serve neither you nor the boy. Take yourselves off before I kill you both." His hand was on his dagger.

Greatly frightened, I edged from the table.

Bear ruffled his beard with deliberate care while eyeing the man with visible—if mute—ill will. Then, with a grunt, he used his large hands to push himself up from the bench. He was a head taller than the man—enough to make the man back away some steps.

"Crispin," Bear called. "We're not wanted here."

"Your kind are not wanted anywhere," declared the man. "Traitors! Be gone with you!"

Quite slowly, Bear walked away from the house, moving in the direction of the road. I stayed close by his side. But knowing all too well the man was behind us—and recalling the dagger—I found it hard not to turn around.

"Crispin!" Bear whispered harshly. "Don't look! It will provoke. Just head for the trees."

"Do you know him?" I asked.

"Only by his face. As he said, he's part of Ball's brother-hood."

We moved to the road, crossed it, and approached the forest. Bear's step continued to be measured, refusing to honor the man by looking back.

I was not so composed. In spite of Bear's warning, I darted a glance back. The man was standing before his house. To my horror, he had a longbow in his hands. Worse, he had nocked an arrow and was pulling back the drawstring.

"Bear!" I shouted. "He's going to shoot at us!"

3

PON THE INSTANT, Bear swung about and shoved me so hard I tumbled. Then he dove down. Even as he did, I heard a sound—*zutt!*

Bear gave a harsh grunt, cried, "Run!" then picked himself up and ran headlong for the protection of the trees.

With Bear hobbling along as best he could, we stumbled into the forest. Once there we continued running for I don't know how long. When at last Bear halted, he leaned against a tree, gasping for breath. He looked at his left arm. I followed his gaze and near swooned: an arrow was sticking through the fleshy part. Blood was trickling down.

"Bear," I cried. "He struck you!"

"Just barely," he said, though his hand was already crimson with blood. "If you had not warned me, I'd be dead."

"Forgive me," I said. "When I said we should stop I only meant—"

"No, no. It's only sweet Jesus—and you—who care for me. Feel free to disobey me at any time."

I gazed back, but could see nothing of the road, the house, or the man. "Do you think he'll follow?"

"That kind will get others first. And then, I promise, they'll follow."

"But wasn't he a friend?"

"Doubt it not; old friends make the worst enemies. I know their secrets and their way of thinking. If they believe I've betrayed them, I've become their worst foe. They won't rest until they kill me. But no more talk," he said, beckoning me toward him. "You must pull the arrow out."

"What do you mean?" I cried.

"Take hold of the end of the arrow, break off the feathered end, then pull the whole thing out."

"Are you . . . sure?" I stammered.

"Crispin," he said, "more men die of wounds than blows to the heart. Quickly, now!" He held out his arm, winglike.

With my stomach churning to the point of illness, I went to him. Bracing myself, I gripped the arrow at the nether ends.

Bear gritted his teeth. "Do it!" he said.

I faltered.

"Crispin," he shouted. "On my life! Break it!"

Hands shaking, I took a deep breath, and broke the arrow.

"*Jesu!*" Bear cried out.

I stood there, panting, feeling faint.

"Now!" he commanded. "Pull it out, pointed end first!"

Grimacing, I did what he told me, then flung the arrow away as if it was some loathsome snake. The effort left me so weak, I leaned against a tree.

Bear, meanwhile, bent over, scooped up some dead leaves, and pressed them against his bleeding arm. It staunched the blood somewhat.

"Will . . . will you be all right?" I managed to say.

"As God wills it," he growled. "I've seen worse for men that lived. We need make haste. I'm sure we'll be pursued." That said, he held out a hand. I helped him up. After shaking himself like a wet dog, he plunged deeper into the forest.

I hurried after, but kept glancing back.

The forest was without tracks or trails. The more we stumbled on, the more I lost my sense of time and place. Stout oak, elm, and ash grew beyond any number I could count. The warp of branches hid the sky. The air was humid, thick with the stench of decay. Tangled bushes clutched our feet. Here and there were boggy mires. All in all, it was an uninviting world, with not the slightest trace of human life.

Bear was constantly clutching his arm, increasingly a-sweat with struggle. Even I was short of breath.

"Shouldn't we seek a path?" I asked after we had labored long.

"The more marked the path," said Bear between heavy panting, "the more likely it will take us to a place others will know. Didn't someone say, 'New lives require new paths'? This way's best."

In faith, I'm not sure who led the way, Bear or I. It might have been the occasional ray of sunlight that gave us direction—fingerposts set down by God on high.

After we had gone for what felt like many leagues, Bear began to falter increasingly until he abruptly halted. "God's heart," he exclaimed. "I can go no more."

All but falling, he sat with his back propped against an oak. His face was drawn, paler than normal. Shivering, he wrapped his cloak tightly round while holding his wounded arm in such a way I knew it was giving him much pain.

"You said the wound was not bad," I said.

"No such thing as a good wound," he muttered, shutting his eyes.

I stood there dismayed. "What shall I do?" I asked.

"All I need is some food, warmth, and a term of peace." He turned toward me without opening his eyes. "If you have any to spare, I would be willing to share."

Not fooled by his raillery, I sat down opposite and waited anxiously for him to do something. Alas, he continued to sit in a state of collapse, breathing deeply, as if he had run a race and lost.

The more he remained there, the more unnerved I became. With the two of us, Bear had always taken the lead. Great in soul, size, and voice as he was, I had never had to wait on him. What kind of freedom had I gained, I wondered, to be so soon on the edge of calamity?

"Are you hungry?" I asked, somewhat lamely.

"I can't remember when I've eaten last," he confessed.

"I can set a trap," I said. He had taught me how. "I'll catch a hare."

"Good lad," he murmured, his breath labored, his eyes still closed. Then he said, "I'm cold."

I stood up. "While I'm gone," I said, "this might help." I set his split hat back on his bald head, and tied it round his cheeks. A poor thing, that hat, but I knew he cherished it as an emblem of his being. When I set it on him, the bells that hung from the two points tinkled; in the forest they made an empty, mocking sound.

I gathered some fallen leaves and spread them over him from his feet to his chest.

"Does that make you any warmer?"

"I'm well planted," he replied. "Just don't let it become an early burial."

"Bear!" I said.

"I jest," he said, but, in faith, it didn't seem that way to me.

"I'll be quick," I said, and started off.

"Crispin!" he called.

"I'm here."

"I'm not prepared to die."

His words struck hard. "What . . . what do you mean?" I said, upset that he should speak that way.

"In Jesus's name, I'm weak. And I've sinned much."

"I've . . . I've never seen you sin," I said.

He took a deep breath and started to speak, but seemed to change his mind. Instead he whispered, "Just don't abandon me."

"By all that's holy, Bear," I returned, "you know I never would. Call with any need. I'll be no farther than a shout."

I stood there, afraid to leave. But when he said no more, I made myself set off in search of a likely spot to place a snare. As I went, I kept thinking how painful it was for me to hear Bear speak of weakness on his part.

For if he was weak, what did that make me?

4

 SEARCHED FOR an open glade where grass grew, knowing that was where rabbits and hares most liked to feed. As God would have it, I soon found a likely spot close by. There, the sun, finding a rent in the canopy of leaves, had kissed the earth as sweetly as a blessing. It was but a few paces across, a soft green sward of bright green grass that invited rest. Respite, however, was not my mission.

As taught by Bear, I found some thin, flexible willow wands and twisted them into a spring trap much like a noose. Trying to touch the twigs as little as possible—lest the beasts sniff out my scent—I set the snare down in the middle of the glade, then took myself off the immediate spot and waited, rock in hand.

Bear had instructed me not to move, to breathe softly; merely, in fact, to think, and to do so silently. But how difficult to wait when you are wanting food and that food is not yet caught—nay, not even visible. For the sound of waiting is full of noise: every creak was hope, every rustle expectation.

I kept mulling over Bear's words—that he had sinned much. I, who loved him as a father, thought of all I knew of him, but could not imagine what forgiveness he might need, save for some small measure of anger or vanity, his daily faults. I could not help but think of how truly short a time I had known Bear, how—save some fragments he'd revealed—little I knew regarding the full measure of his life. Still, Bear's condition made me aware how large was my dependence on him, how small I was alone. What, I kept asking myself, if he grew worse? How I cursed myself for urging him to stop at the alestake!

Then and there I swore—by my Saint Giles—a

sacred vow: As Bear had taken care of me I would care for him. I could not be a boy. I *must* be a man!

"Lord Jesus!" I prayed with all my heart, my eyes full of tears. "Give me the strength to help Bear. Give Bear the strength to live."

Despite my intent, exhaustion caused me to nod off only to wake with a start, brought back from sleep by the frantic thrashing of a small hare tangled in my snare. I leaped up and grabbed the rock that had fallen from my lap. Diving flat out onto my belly, I snatched the beast, and despite its frantic kicking, brained it. It died with the stroke.

With pride in my triumph, I took the hare by its bloody ears and carried it back to Bear. I found him asleep, the leaves I'd provided for cover scattered. But at least his wound had clotted.

Not wanting to disturb him, I removed flint and tinder from our sack and began a fire. It wasn't long before the hare was roasting on a spit. The smell caused my hunger to gnaw at me.

Bear stirred, then woke but only stared at me with glazed eyes. "You did well," he whispered.

"As you taught me."

"You were gone so long . . . I thought you had snared trouble, or that—God protect us—trouble . . .

had snared you." His face glistened with sweat.

"Does your wound hurt?"

"It throbs."

My heart tightened. I touched fingers to his brow. It was very hot. "Is it a fever?"

"Merely hunger," he said as if to tease me, but his unusual mildness undercut his levity.

Wanting to hasten the cooking, I threw more wood onto the fire. The flame flared. The meat turned dark, the smell of it making my mouth water. When the hare was cooked I tore the carcass apart and gave Bear the pieces.

At first he ate—one-handed—with rapacious hunger, which pleased me. Alas, he soon stopped. "You must feed me," he said.

Though it upset me to do it, I nonetheless did as he bid, like some chick stuffing food into the maw of its much larger parent.

"Yourself, too," he murmured.

"I'm fine." In truth, I was famished, but I allowed myself just one mouthful. I made him take the rest.

When he'd done, I said, "Do you feel better?"

"Somewhat."

I knelt by his side and studied him. He was dreadful pale. His breathing was thick.

I could see for myself that he was sinking. So was my heart.

Not knowing what else to do, I said, "I'll try and get another hare."

"As you will," he mumbled.

I stood up.

"Crispin," he whispered. "There are private things I need to say."

God's truth: I didn't want to know such things. But the pain in his voice held me. "You need your sleep," I said in haste.

"Yes," he said. "I do." And drifted off to what I hoped was only sleep.

I wanted to get help but hardly knew where to take my first step, much less which way to aim. In the end, unwilling to leave him, I stayed by his side.

Night came with lowering clouds enough to hide all stars. The only light was the smoldering cinders of our dwindling fire. I took it to be an augury of Bear's life.

Heart full of pain, I went on my knees and prayed to my patron, Saint Giles, that he might help Bear. I pledged I'd do anything and everything if he blessed Bear with strength. Even so, in the heart of my being, my fear was growing that Bear was fated—it choked me just to give it name—to die.

With that fear came a greater fear: if Bear died I didn't know what to do. Where could I go? What would I be?

Unable to answer, I felt that the freedom I'd so recently won was melting like a spent candle.

What followed was a long and doleful night. The forest creaked and groaned as if an encircling doom was laying siege to Bear. When I slept—which I did but fitfully—my frightful dreams were equal to my waking worries. I took the dreams as dismal warnings. Sure enough, by dawn's first light, I could see that Bear had turned worse.

Though exhausted, I knew I should act quickly. Yet, despite new and desperate prayers, I had no notion what to do. I stirred up the fire, but beyond that I could only wait and watch my friend, my heart raw with naked helplessness.

But as I sat there, I began to realize that the forest had grown uncommon still—as if it held its breath. Gradually, I began to sense something amiss, as though something was slithering near.

I leaped up and searched about but saw nothing save the creeping shadows of the dawning forest. Even so, I was convinced a thing was there, a thing drawing nigh.

The hairs on the back of my neck began to prickle. My heart pounded. I could hardly breathe. For I recalled a notion I'd heard: that when the Angel of Death slips in to snatch a soul, all sounds, all movements, cease.

Next moment I realized that there were eyes, eyes peering out of the woods, eyes gazing right at us, large eyes, dark and brown, fixed and staring. Nothing but eyes, detached from any corporal body, as if part of some advancing ghost.

Oh, blessed Lord who gives all life—I thought—*it's Death, Death himself who has come for Bear!*

5

RADUALLY, DIMLY, I perceived a figure hidden by the leaves. Even so, it was only eyes that held me with an unblinking gaze. Was what I saw of *this* world or another?

Greatly shocked, I turned toward the sleeping Bear, then shifted hastily back. Slowly, I realized it was a small person looking out at us. The next moment I grasped that it was a *child*—but whether a *human* or not, I was uncertain.

The face was obscured by grime and long, snarled

brown hair. Impossible, too, to distinguish clothing, muted and rent as it was, as if part of the foliage.

I returned the stare, but the child did no more than remain still, eyes steady as stone upon us. The longer the gaze held, the greater grew my fright. I tried desperately to think what Bear would do.

"Be off with you!" I cried, raising an arm and taking a step forward.

When the child made no response, I asked, "Who are you?"

No answer.

Seeing a stout branch upon the ground, I snatched it up and held it like a club that I might defend myself and Bear—if it came to that.

The child remained in place.

Brandishing the stick as if to strike, I took another step. This time the child retreated, noiselessly, as if floating above the earth.

"Are you of this world?" I shouted. "In God's name tell me who and what you are!"

Abruptly, the child turned and scampered off among the trees, and, for all that I could see, vanished.

My fears grew. If what I saw was human, and he went to tell others about us, matters could turn worse. But if what I saw was a spirit, what devilish harm might he bring down upon us?

I knelt by Bear's side.

"Bear," I said. "We've been found. There may be danger coming. We need to move!"

He opened his eyes. It was, at best, a foggy gape and conveyed no understanding. I was not even sure he knew I had spoken.

I put my hand to his face: hot and sticky with sweat. I had no doubt he was being consumed by the rankest of humors. The wound had taken full hold, poisoning his whole body.

"Bear!" I cried. "We must move!"

His reply was a moan of such despair it struck terror to the deepest regions of my soul. Distraught, I stood up and looked into the forest in hopes I'd see a sign of the strange child. The child was gone. Belatedly, I knew I should have begged for help.

I tried to pull at Bear, to make him stand, but his weight and bulk proved too great.

In panic, I searched round for a heavier stick with which, if came the need, I could make some defense. Finding one, I stood on guard before Bear, my heart pounding.

The forest was mute. No one came.

Still wondering what I'd see—someone real or unreal, friend or foe—I stirred the flame but kept looking round. Just how much time passed I don't know, but as unexpectedly as before, the child—if child it was—returned.

Again, what first I saw were eyes gazing at me from deep among the bushes.

I jumped up. When the child did not shift, I called out, "In God's name will you help us?" and moved forward. Even as I did, I heard another sound. I spun about.

A second person had appeared.

6

HE NEWCOMER was a woman, or so I took her to be, for she was aged to the point of being unsexed. Cronelike, bent almost double as if loaded down with the weight of years, her head was twisted to one side in the manner of a listening bird. Frail and small—smaller than I—her garments were foul rags, tattered and torn. Her skin was begrimed, her long hair gray, greasy, and unkempt, akin to the shredded moss that dangled from the trees. Her nose was beakish, while her

mouth, etched round with multiple lines like so many needled stitches, fell in on toothless gums. Fingers were rough and misshapen, with long, clawlike and thick, yellow nails.

Though her wrinkled face had stiff, white hairs upon her chin, most striking of all was her left eye: glazed over with a lifeless, milky white, a sure sign of blindness. Her right eye seemed the larger, brighter too, with the deepest, most penetrating gaze I ever saw. Is this hag, I wondered, the bearer of the evil eye?

"Who . . . who are you?" I cried, backing toward Bear, determined to protect him. "What do you want of us?"

The old woman slowly lifted an arm and pointed her gnarled fingers at Bear. "Troth says—the man is ill." She spoke with a clogged and broken voice, her toothless mouth continually munching.

"Who is Troth?" I asked, bewildered.

By way of answering, the old woman turned and gestured with a hand. The child I'd first seen stepped into the clearing. I saw now that she was a girl. Though shorter than me and much younger than the crone, she was garbed in similar motley rags. Whereas the woman was old, bent, and ugly, the girl was not misshapen. But her mouth! *Dear God!* It was cleft—grotesquely disfigured and twisted, shaped like a hare's mouth.

The girl's appearance was so dreadful I must have gawked. In haste, she pulled her tangled hair across the lower half of her face, veil-like, to hide her gross disfigurement.

I made a quick decision: no matter that these folk were outlandish—there was no one else to whom I could turn. "He's hurt," I said, indicating Bear. "Can you aid him?"

"Aude coaxes man to life," said the woman, her good eye appraising Bear. "Aude keeps them in life. Bring him." She turned as if to go.

"Who is Aude?" I called.

"Me," muttered the hag, making finger movements at the girl. The girl edged forward, moving with great skittishness, eyes avoiding mine, like a fearful dog.

I went to one side of Bear. "I can't move him," I said. "He's too big. Heavy." I spoke loudly, simply, as if the hag were deaf.

The old woman lifted both hands and clasped them. The girl, with some kind of understanding, went to Bear's other side.

Troth—for so I gathered the girl's name to be—made some guttural sound. It was not human talk—not in any proper sense. It sounded as if it came from her throat, animal-like. While unsettling, I took it to mean we were to lift.

The girl's strength surprised me. Between the two of us, we managed to get Bear up. Perhaps Bear also worked, for when upright he opened his eyes a slit. I snatched up our sack, and we began to follow the old woman.

As we went along, it occurred to me that the woman's way and manner—slow, shuffling, hunched over—had something witchlike to it. And the girl, with her odd, split mouth and her wariness, was just as odd. But at that moment—may God forgive me!—in order to help Bear, I would have embraced the Devil.

7

HE GIRL AND I, supporting Bear from either side, clumsily followed the old woman as she picked her way slowly through the woods. Though I would have never found where they took us on my own, we did not go far. It was not a true dwelling in any sense I knew—rather, it was the crudest of shelters, a space between two boulders over which some boughs had been set to form a roof. A wall of wattle

obscured the entryway with bushes, arranged so a passerby would not likely notice what was there. It was well hidden.

Yet once I came round that screening wall, I saw that the living space was not so different from the poor dwellings I knew in my own village of Stromford. Matted leaves and crumbling rushes covered a dirt floor while two heaps of straw appeared to serve as sleeping places. A smoldering fire burned within a ring of soot-blackened stones. From the crude roof hung drying plants and herbs. Among them I spied mistletoe, which alarmed me for I knew it was used in magic spells.

On the ground were two rusty iron pots that looked to be old soldiers' helmets. Three chipped wooden cups lay nearby. There were mazers, too, plus a few closed linen sacks. If I had seen skulls, I would not have been surprised.

The old woman made a motion with her hand, which I took to be telling us she wanted Bear placed on one of the straw pallets. The girl and I did what she asked, though Bear mostly tumbled into a heap.

Making a rolling motion of her hand, the woman said, "Over."

On my knees, grunting with effort, I turned Bear so he lay upon his back.

The woman, hovering near, made another gesture, turning her hand so the palm faced down, then lowering it slightly.

Were these gestures a casting of spells?

But the girl seemed to make sense of them. She took Bear's good arm and straightened it. Moving his wounded arm caused him to moan. She did the same with his legs. Then she covered Bear to his neck with his robe as well as a tattered blanket they had, leaving his wounded arm exposed. In all of this, the girl worked with a slow, practiced touch.

The hag stood over Bear, staring down. Then she reached out and fingered his cap. Abruptly, she turned her good eye to me. "Who wounded him with an arrow?" she asked in a voice so broken it was all but indistinct.

"How . . . how did you know?"

"Though Aude has only one good eye she can see," she said. "What befell him?" Her gaze was hard on me. "He was also beaten, many times." She pulled Bear's blanket back and pointed to red marks across his chest. "Burn marks. Who did these things?"

"I'm . . . not certain," I said, uneasy about how much of our history I should reveal.

After staring at Bear for a long moment, she suddenly

rasped, "Nerthus wants life to live. Aude will try to help." A nod and the girl covered Bear again.

Who this *Nerthus* was, I had no idea.

Again the old woman faced the girl, opened her hand—palm up—and lifted it slightly. Then she moved that same right hand as if she were squeezing something, only to put the hand to her own cheek. Finally, she pointed to the branches hanging from the roof.

"Sorrel," she muttered. "Marigold. Bark. Barley." At the last she pointed to a sack and rubbed her hands together as if washing.

Troth plucked some leaves from the branches that hung above. She crumpled brittle bits into one of the iron helmets, then added pieces of bark. From one of the bags she took up a handful of barley and threw it in, too. That done, she carried the helmet outside.

"Where's she going?" I asked. Everything they did made me fearful.

"Water."

"Why doesn't she speak?"

The old woman shifted round to look at me with her one good eye. "Troth was born with a broken mouth," she muttered. "People fear her. So Troth speaks little. Besides," she added, peering up at me in her twisted way,

"Aude's gods say: The less that's said, the more that's understood."

"Can she hear?" I asked, staring after the girl.

"Troth listens to Aude's hands," was the crone's grudging reply.

The woman stuck her bony fingers into a small clay pot, which was filled with what appeared to be some kind of grease along with the smell of honey.

Clutching me for support, Aude went on her knees, and began to apply the ointment to Bear's wound, his limbs, neck, and face. Hearing her mumble under her breath, I wondered if she were conjuring magic.

Alarmed, I gazed about in search of a cross, something, anything Christian.

I saw none.

"Good dame," I blurted out, "are you . . . a Christian?"

My question made the hag pause in her work. She drew back on her haunches. Her frowning silence made me regret my question. After a while she said, "Why do you ask?"

"I . . . I fear for his soul."

She fixed me fiercely with her eye. "Nay, it's Aude . . . you fear."

My face grew hot. "A . . . little," I allowed.

"Oh, yes," she said, gnawing on her toothless gums,

"Aude is old. Aude is ugly. Aude . . . and Troth . . . live apart. Do you fear such things, boy?"

"Y . . . yes."

"Know then," she said, "that Aude is of the old religion."

"*Old* religion?" I cried, taken aback. "What do you mean?"

"The old gods—it's they Aude worships."

Shocked, for I had never ever heard anyone speak of "old gods," I hardly knew what to say.

Her single eye remained sharp on me. "Do you still want Aude's help?"

"In Jesus's name," I whispered, "I want him well."

"Nerthus—my god—gives life," she said. "What can you give?"

"What . . . do you . . . want?" I stammered, fearful that she might request my soul.

"It's for you to offer."

"I have . . . very little," I said. "A few pennies."

The crone held out a clawlike hand.

I went to Bear's sack, scraped up our few remaining coins, and dropped them in her withered palm. She curled crumpled fingers over them and put them in a little bag tied round her waist with a leather thong.

"Old Aude shall try for life," she muttered, and resumed daubing her grease mix on Bear's limbs.

Afraid to press her further, my mouth dry with apprehension, I watched in silence. The dimness of the bower; the ruby-colored fire-glow; her ancient, tangled look; her multi-hued rags; her broken posture—all made the crone appear like some deep-wood demon, and the girl, with her disfigured face, an ill-begotten familiar.

Silently, I made urgent prayers, begging my all-powerful Lord that though this woman was not Christian, she might help my Bear.

8

ROTH CAME and set the heated helmet down next to the old woman. Spiraling vapors—like drifting spirits—curled up.

"Lift his head," Aude whispered.

I did as she bid. The old woman squeezed Bear's cheeks so hard his mouth gaped opened. Troth, using the mazer, poured in some liquid. Bear gagged, coughed, but swallowed. This was repeated a few times.

"He must rest," said Aude.

In the dim light we sat in silence watching Bear. Then the crone abruptly shifted round, leaned toward me and said, "You must tell Aude who you are."

Alarmed, I managed to say, "What do you mean?"

"You are fleeing."

"What . . . what makes you think so?"

"You are alone in the forest with nothing save your fear. He wears a juggler's cap, but here you cannot sing and dance for coins. An arrow has wounded him. He has been abused. You were hiding. You must tell of these things to Aude and Troth."

I was afraid to say I didn't trust her.

"It will help," Aude said.

"How?"

"To know how a man suffers, is to know how he lives . . . or dies."

I glanced at Troth. The girl was staring at me, her dark brown eyes unfathomable. As for her covered mouth—why should it so trouble me?

Then I remembered: in my village of Stromford it was said that if, before a babe was born, the Devil came and touched the mother's swollen belly, the babe's limb or hand or face—like Troth's—would bear the Devil's evil mark.

Even as I stared at her, that knowledge chilled my heart.

A tap on my leg startled me. It was the woman. "You must speak."

I felt trapped. Not knowing what else to do, I took a deep breath and told my tale.

I revealed how, not long ago, I, a new-made orphan, fled my little village because I'd been proclaimed a wolf's head—meaning anyone was free to kill me.

How a kind God led me to Bear, a juggler, who became in turn, master, teacher, protector, and then, as I would have it, the father I never knew.

How we traveled together until we came to the city of Great Wexly, where I discovered I was the illegitimate son of one Lord Furnival, a knight of the realm. There, I also discovered Bear was a spy for John Ball's brotherhood.

How my enemies captured Bear, and tortured him in hopes of making him to reveal where I was.

How I, to ransom Bear's liberty, renounced any claim to my noble name, and by doing so, Bear and I were able to pass out of Great Wexly to our freedom.

How, finally, Bear was wounded by a man who believed he had betrayed Ball's brotherhood.

At first I told all this haltingly. But as I went on, it ran from me like water from a broken bowl. When done I was in tears. For I, in a manner of speaking, was a listener too. How extraordinary that I, who but a short time ago never knew a life beyond the passing of repetitious days, could tell a tale of being, doing, and becoming.

Though Aude and Troth had listened to me closely, neither spoke, nor asked questions, nor made so much as one remark, hearing my words in solemn silence.

By the time I finished the day was gone. Shadow filled the bower. The air was cool and hushed. I was weary in heart and bone. With Bear sleeping easier than before, I could not help myself—and nodded off.

I woke with a start. A dim, ruddy light suffused the bower. My first sensation was fear, thinking I'd fallen into the place of damnation that all true Christians fear. Then I realized the redness was naught but the shimmering embers of the bower fire.

I swung round and bent over Bear. He was asleep, barely breathing. I put a hand to his face. Still hot. I touched his arm. He pulled it away as though stung.

Looking round, I searched for the old woman and the girl. I did not see them, but saw that the front of the bower was bathed in soft, white light. I gazed at it, puzzled, until I realized it was moonlight.

As I listened I caught a faint sound from beyond. On hands and knees I crept to the walled-in entrance of the bower and peeked out.

Aude stood before the bower in an open space that was dappled by moonlight. Kneeling by her side was Troth. A teasing breeze tossed their tangled garments. Tree leaves stirred as though sifting secrets.

Aude had one raised hand and was dangling a branch of mistletoe. The other hand gripped the girl's shoulder, as if for support.

In a slow, broken voice, the hag was chanting:

> *There flowed a spring*
> *Beneath a hawthorn tree*
> *That once had a cure for sorrow.*
> *Beside the spring and the tree*
> *Now stands a young girl*
> *Who's full of love, this girl,*
> *Held fast by love, this girl.*
> *So whoever seeks true love*
> *Will not find it in the spring,*
> *But in this girl,*
> *This girl,*
> *Who stands by the hawthorn tree.*

As I watched and listened, I had no doubt it was some kind of enchantment. Were they trying to steal Bear's soul? My own? If these people were indeed spirit folk, if the crone was a true witch, we should not, must not stay. Yet how could we go if Bear was so ill? Once again came the questions: What should I do if he died? How would I be able to stay free?

I asked this of myself so often it all but became a plainsong chant, to which I provided the only answer I could summon: I must think and act as a man.

But how?

9

ORNING'S DULL LIGHT nudged me into wakefulness. I opened my eyes but lay still, listening, trying to take measure of where I was, of what was happening. What I heard was a steady *shhhh* sound, which I gradually recognized as rain. I recalled my sighting of the old woman and the girl during the night—chanting in the moon glow. I felt a chill.

Easing up one elbow, I peered about. Rainwater dripped

down through the leafy roof, making a constant, *pat pat pat*. The bower floor had turned muddy in spots while rocks to either side glistened wetly. The fire was cold, the ashes white. The constant dripping sounds made me tense.

Across the way from me, on the other pile of straw, the old woman lay asleep, her toothless mouth agape. Her breath was raspy. Troth was curled by her side—cat and kitten.

On my knees I studied Bear's face. He seemed to be in peace, breathing with greater regularity. No sweat was on his brow. The redness on his wound had abated somewhat. But when I touched fingers to his brow it was still too warm.

Hearing a sound, I swung about. The girl had woken. She was staring at me. When I returned the look she pulled her hair across her face in that gesture that hid her disfigurement—her Devil's mark. Our eyes held.

"Can you speak?" I said.

No reply.

"Can you?"

"Ugah," she said, or some such sound.

I pointed to one of my ears. "Hear?"

She nodded yes.

"And your name is . . . Troth."

"Oth."

A hand to my chest. "My name is Crispin."

"Ispin."

I pointed at the old woman. "Aude."

Another nod.

"Mother?"

No response.

"Is she your mother?" I tried.

The girl shook her head.

"And . . . your father?"

No reply. Her face was like an empty mask.

"Are you . . . Christian?"

Again no reply. Then I recalled what people said, that demons and witches recoiled from a visible sign of the cross. I held up my hands and made one with my fingers.

She returned a look absent of emotion or any hint of knowing. Still—I noted—she had not cringed. And though yet uncertain what she was, I reminded myself that she had helped Bear.

"May Jesus," I said, "grant you a blessing for being kind to my friend."

She continued to fix her gaze on me. But this time, she shifted her hair so it was no longer covering her disfigured mouth: as if she wanted me to see, *dared* me to see. That confused me. Was she showing me her evilness? I made myself hold my gaze while inwardly saying protective prayers.

Then, to break the moment, I pointed to *my* mouth. "Hungry," I said and patted my stomach.

She made another guttural sound, got up and leaned over the fire, blowing on the coals till they flamed. She put some wood on. The fire blazed. She set a helmet on it and added a handful of something. Now and again she stirred.

Frustrated by my inability to make any clear sense of her, I kept watch over Bear. *Tell me what to do!* I kept thinking. As God's mercy would have it, his eyes fluttered open.

"Crispin," he whispered, "where are you?"

I leaned over him. "Here."

"What . . . is this place?"

"Deep in the forest. Where a crone and a girl live. They're tending to you." Then I bent down and whispered into his ear. "Bear, I don't know who or what they are. Except, they aren't Christians."

He made a feeble effort to get up only to fall back. His eyes closed. He slept.

Ill at ease, I looked over my shoulder. Troth was stirring

her pot, but I sensed she'd been watching me. Had she heard my words?

She scooped up what she had been cooking, put it in a bowl, and offered it to me. It appeared to be cooked oats. *Was it safe to eat?* I wondered.

Troth made an impatient gesture to her mouth—as if urging me to eat.

Though fearful of her food, my stomach begged. The last time I had eaten was when I took that morsel of hare I'd cooked for Bear. Unable to resist, I closed my eyes, made a prayer for my safety, used my fingers to scoop up the food, and shoved it into my mouth.

Nothing untoward happened.

All that damp, warm day Bear remained asleep on the straw, though now and again he tossed about. I had hopes that he was mending, but being so uneasy, I remained by his side, on guard, keeping a wary eye on Troth and Aude.

The rain continued, a steady, sopping rain. At times thunder rolled, and crackling lightning sucked all color from the air, turning the world a ghostly white. Humid air was thick with the sweet smells of wood and decaying leaves, mingling with the pungent herbs that hung within the bower.

Once, while I looked on, and the old woman worked on Bear, she suddenly squeezed where the arrow had entered Bear's arm. A spurt of dark blood and yellow pus erupted, and with it a splinter of wood. I gagged with disgust. But Aude snatched up the splinter and, muttering incomprehensibly, flung it in the fire, then went back and salved Bear's wound anew.

I felt gratitude that she took from him something that was ill. In truth, I was finding it increasingly difficult to deny that no matter what or who these people were, they were not acting wickedly.

Dare I show them gratitude?

10

EAR SLEPT ON.

As time passed, Aude and Troth seemed to do very little. The girl plucked leaves from the herbs and ground them into powder in a stone pestle. Once she went into the woods and foraged food. Once, she returned with toadstools, which I knew were unfit for humans. She ate them nonetheless. I was shocked.

The hag sat mostly by the fire as if looking into it, communing with it. Sometime I heard her croon as she rocked back and forth. Now and again she attended Bear. Then she and Troth—with a little help from me—fed him their brew and salved his wound.

By dusk, the rain had slackened. Daylight faded. Everything felt strange, ill-measured, and misplaced. A corpse-gray mist wormed among the knobby roots of trees. Now and again a bird called, its sharp trill weaving through the dim gray light like a lost thread of silver. A fox appeared at the bower entryway, its fur a wet and mottled rusty hue. It stood without apparent fear, sharp nose sniffing quizzically, ears erect, one foot up. Aude took no notice. Troth did. She went to the beast, knelt, and rubbed its ears, after which the fox trotted off. A few times birds flew into the bower, hopped about and pecked.

It was all so fantastical I was convinced these were bewitched people—if they were truly people.

And yet, and yet, they seemed kind.

Once, when Troth went to fetch more wood, and Aude was tending to Bear and therefore close to me, I said, "Is Troth your daughter?"

She considered momentarily before shaking her head.

"Then . . . how did she come to you?"

"Her mother died when giving birth. The father, seeing that face, pronounced her Devil's work and would not keep her. No one would. But Aude took Troth and let her live."

I said, "How was she able to touch that fox?"

"Creatures do not fear her. Humans do." She leaned toward me so that I felt skewered by her one good eye. "But then men fear most what they understand least. Ignorance," she hissed, "makes fear."

"What do you mean?" I said, wondering if she thought *me* ignorant.

She turned away, leaving me to brood upon her words.

Not till next day did Bear truly wake. That's to say, he opened his eyes and pushed himself up a bit with his good arm. Much weight had been lost. His face was gaunt, his small eyes dark rimmed.

I went to his side.

"How long have we been here?" he asked, as if rising from a long, deep sleep.

"Two days."

He shook his great head, looked about, scratched his red beard, and rubbed his bald pate. "I've little memory of coming," he said.

Trying to move his wounded arm, he winced and lay back down, eyes closed.

"Are you hungry?" I asked.

"A bear is always hungry," he whispered with a welcome hint of smile, though his eyes remained shut.

"He wants to eat," I called to Aude.

She and Troth came to his side bringing a mazer of broth.

Bear opened his eyes and gazed up at the old woman. "Good morrow," he said.

Aude stared at him.

"May the blessing of Jesus be with you for your kindness," Bear murmured.

Making no reply, but working silently, Aude and Troth fed him. When done, they withdrew.

"How far have we come from Great Wexly?" he asked when I returned to his side.

"We had already walked some time when the arrow struck you. Even then we went on. Bear," I whispered into his ear, "I don't know what these people are. They have been kind . . . But they're strange. Not like anyone I've known. I don't know if we should trust them. Perhaps we should go on."

"Where?"

"Anyplace."

He shook his head. "John Ball's brotherhood is everywhere. They've marked me as a traitor and—"

"What?"

"As long as we're not discovered, we should be fine. Besides, I can't travel."

"But—"

"Patience, Crispin. Patience." He lay back, closed his eyes. Then he said, "I wish a priest was near."

"Why?"

He sighed, swallowed hard then said, "Crispin, like most men, I've done things that . . . need God's mercy and forgiveness."

I gazed at him. It was what he had suggested before. And as before, if there was something he needed to confess, I was uncertain I wanted to hear. "Shall . . . shall I try to find a priest?" I asked.

"No," he whispered. "I'm not ready." He was silent for a while. Then he said, "Once I knew a man who owned a great bear. This man kept this bear cruelly with a chain, so as to make him dance at will. For years he kept that beast, bragging he'd tamed him, though he never turned his back. Then one day, he *did* turn his back and the bear smote him dead. But the bear let me—who had been kind to him— cut that chain. When I did, the bear lumbered off."

"What am I to learn from that?"

"I took my name from that bear."

"Why?"

"That bear knew when it was time to free himself."

"I don't understand."

"Because," he whispered, "that bear was held back from his natural state, as if . . . as if the links of the chain were his sins. My sins bind me—just so."

I felt increasingly uncomfortable. "Bear," I blurted out, "I don't want to know your sins!"

He closed his eyes. "To love a man," he whispered, "you must know his failings."

That said, he closed his eyes and slept.

I withdrew, greatly troubled. But then, I trusted myself—a gift from Bear—to know right from wrong. I would not, could not allow myself to think of Bear in any way but as goodness itself. How could he have done bad things? No, I didn't want to know.

How hard it was for me to discern when evil clothed itself in goodness, or when there might be a kernel of goodness within the chaff of evil. Then I recalled what Aude had said: *Ignorance made fear.* But my thought was—as I looked at Bear and pondered what he'd said—if ignorance gave comfort, I would rather cleave to that.

11

EAR CONTINUED to mend. Now and again he sat up, but it was a struggle for him to move. His arm still ailed. Now and again he laughed, always a measure of his health. Best of all, I could see that each passing day brought him strength.

Though he tried to talk to Troth, she kept apart. As for Aude, she paid Bear little mind but went about her mumbling motions.

Occasionally, Troth tried to teach me some hand signs, gestures that seemed to mean *go*, or *come*, or *more*. It seemed to please her when we communicated that way.

Thus did our days pass. I felt as if I were being held in some formless time and place, tottering between worlds I could neither see nor grasp nor fully understand.

I kept thinking that, though Bear was far from recovered, we should leave. Surely it was wrong to stay with such folk. Perhaps it was a sin. Every day we did not go, my tension grew: Would Bear never get fully well? Had they put him under a spell? Were they—in fact—holding us?

One day Troth was gone from morning till night, but

when she returned she had some rough cloth. As I was to learn much later, she had purchased it (I knew not where) with the pennies I had given Aude. Under the tutelage of the old woman, the girl fashioned the cloth into rough breeches and a kirtle for Bear.

He was pleased. I, recalling his blue-and-red leggings, his pointy shoes of better days, was not as pleased. Still, I tried to tell myself that it might bring us a little closer to leaving.

Now and again, Aude and Troth left the bower for periods of time. Whenever they walked out, Aude kept a hand on Troth's shoulder. She was that dependent on the girl. Though they stayed away all day, they did not tell us where they were going.

Then for an entire night they were gone. When they returned the next morning I was startled to see what looked to be blood on Aude's garments. It alarmed me greatly. After all, I had never seen them with meat of any kind, only the plants Troth found in the woods. What kind of blood rituals might they have done?

I crept to Bear's side.

"Bear," I whispered, "did you see the blood on Aude?"

He nodded.

"What can it mean?"

"I don't know."

"Bear," I said to him, "surely you must know now we're in great danger."

"I *don't* know. What makes you think so?"

"These people . . . I suspect they are . . . witches."

His look seemed to suppress a smile. "Have you questioned them?" he asked.

"Of course not!"

"Perhaps I should, then."

Feeling he spoke as if I were a child, I quit his side and kept to myself. What kind of freedom, thought I, did I have if it meant I was always bound by his decisions?

Later on, I lay with my head cushioned in my arms, feeling drowsy. Troth was busy with her herbs. Aude sat before the smoldering fire. Bear pulled himself from the bed of old straw and sat opposite the woman, across the flames. After a goodly while, I heard him say, "Old dame, may I ask a question?"

Aude mumbled her assent.

"Might that," said Bear, "be stains of blood upon your garments?"

Across the bower Troth stopped her work and looked around. I dared not move but listened closely.

"It is," I heard the woman say.

"Have you been hurt?" said Bear. He spoke gently.

At first Aude said nothing to this. Then she muttered, "Aude practices midwifery."

"Ah!" cried Bear. "Then you helped deliver a woman of a babe."

She nodded.

"And all was well?"

"It was."

Bear was quiet for a moment. Then he said, "Where would this have happened?" asked Bear.

"In the village."

"A village!" said Bear. "I had no idea one was near."

"A few leagues."

"Does it have a name?"

"Chaunton."

"I never heard of the place. Do they call on you often?"

Aude seemed to consider the question. Then she said, "There is no Christian priest in Chaunton. There is only a bailiff, who lords over all and even preaches to the people. Falsely so, they tell Aude in secret, for they fear him. That bailiff rejects Aude. Spits on Aude. Calls Aude pagan. Tells people that Troth is evil. Warns them not to use Aude, lest they lose their souls."

"But all the same, they call on you," said Bear.

"The women do. And some men."

"And you help them in their time."

"Aude has the hands, the skill, and a belt that's never been fastened."

"Then you are much blessed," said Bear. "And does Troth assist you?"

"Aude is very old. More and more Nerthus calls to her. Aude shall go to her soon. Aude is teaching Troth all she knows. Troth will take Aude's place."

Only when Aude and Troth slept did I dare question Bear. "Why does Aude use a belt?" I asked.

"An open belt laid on the birthing woman's belly gives her ease. But then, opening all closed things in her dwelling can help, too. I assure you, Crispin, it's common wisdom. The town is blessed to have Aude near."

"But, Bear," I burst out, "what *are* these people?

He looked at me, smiled and only said, "Kind."

"Aude spoke of a town close by," I pressed. "You said yourself we're not far enough away from Great Wexly. The longer we stay, the more likely we'll be discovered."

This time Bear considered my words seriously. "As for that . . . you may be right," he said. "While I would have preferred to wait and regain all my strength, I suppose we should leave soon."

"Where could we go?"

"Do you remember that road we were on?"

I nodded.

"I think it would have delivered us toward Scotland."

"Is that a good place?"

"For all I care," he said, "that road could take us to the land of the Great Chan. What matters is that we keep our liberty."

"Bear, lead us wherever you want. You've been everywhere."

"I assure you," he returned, "my *everywhere* is not God's *everyplace.*" With a stubby finger he drew crude lines in the bower's mud.

"Here," he said with a jab, "sits the realm of Edward's England. For walking, there's Wales to the west. That's closest of all. Alas, the love of English is rather meager there, and they speak a language I don't know.

"As for Scotland, where we can also walk, that's to the far north, here. The pity is they speak a knapped warp of English tongue. More importantly, they have been our enemies for endless years in useless wars. Thank old Edward Long Shanks for that. Now, then," he went on, "England is an island."

"It is?"

"In the name of Saint Augustine!" cried Bear, "there are times I forget the depth of your ignorance. Yes, England is an island. And the world beyond is very large. Well, then," he continued, "all round England sits deep sea."

"Bear . . ."

"What?"

"What is . . . *sea?*"

Bear looked at me with astonishment. Next moment he broke into boisterous laughter, his first great laugh since being ill. "Oh, God!" he cried looking heavenward, "who hath *all* wisdom, I pray You lend—You need not *give*—just *lend* one eyelash of Your wisdom to this most ignorant of boys."

"Bear!" I cried, quite abashed.

"Forgive me, Crispin. It's not your fault. I mock no man's ignorance, but his ignorance of his ignorance.

"The *sea*, Crispin, is water—also called *ocean*—which covers the world in greater magnitude than land."

"You mock me," I said, scoffing at such an absurdity.

He lifted up his good right hand. "I swear it's true," he said. "Someday, perhaps, you'll go to the sea and measure its depth with your own toes. And Crispin, this ocean is not just vast, but second only to God in power, so that in winter it hurls mighty storms one day in three. In summer, one in ten. As Heaven knows, many a man sails to sea in a leaky cog and never touches dry land again."

I sighed. The more I came to know of the world, the more I knew I knew it not.

"Now, Crispin," Bear went on, returning to his mud sketch, "sail your fat cog upon the sea this way—east—and there's France. All we'll find there is war and devastation. Satan's playing fields. May good Jesus keep us from that.

"Now, there's Flanders, here, east as well, but I don't put trust in such a mercantile people.

"Further north and west is a land—some say—that's all but beyond the world. A land of ice, it's called Iceland. But so cold no kings or lords will rule there. They live without government. Or war. But that seems too fantastical.

"Go south, here, and back across the ocean. You'll find the Kingdoms of Navarre and Castile. Alas for the over-reaching folk of Babel, they too speak a language I don't know.

"Cross the sea *this* way—westerly beyond Wales—there's Ireland. Some say it's a savage place, but I've heard honest men say otherwise. That attracts me."

"Is the world so truly vast?" I asked, amazed by what he had drawn.

"Aye," he said, "and much more still unknown to me.

And Crispin," he said, leaning into my ear and whispering, "some say it's all guarded by dragons."

"Dragons!" I said, staring at his grinning face. "Bear, I've never even heard of these places. Have they . . . Christian peoples?"

"Some, I suppose, have infidels."

"Bear, we need to go someplace that's free from all danger."

"I doubt such exists. In any case, I've not yet the strength to go too far."

"Bear," I said, "you think I'm too young to give advice. But I'm fearful that we'll be found. The old woman spoke of a nearby village. We *need* to leave before we're found."

He lay back and closed his eyes. "You may be right."

"But—"

"Just give me a little more time, Crispin."

Certain I was right, I took it upon myself to find a way to make him go the sooner. Bear would then see I was not the child he thought me. If he was too weak to make decisions, then I would have to make them for us.

12

A FEW DAYS LATER, when the sun was high in the sky, Troth rushed into the bower. She went right to Aude, and made some of her sounds into the old woman's ear. She also made fists of her hands and clenched them, signing. Her urgency made me watch closely.

The old woman nodded. Even as she did, a man appeared at the bower entryway.

Startled—for aside from Aude and Troth, we had seen no others since we'd gone into the forest— I moved toward Bear, ready for the worst.

The man was in his older days: that's to say, of some fifty years, grizzled, and slight. From his garb I saw he was a peasant. He wore a dirty, belted, brown wool tunic that reached his knees, ragged sleeves that almost touched his wrists, plus a back-pointed hood. Leather straps bound his leggings of cloth. He must have been running, for he was all of a sweat, panting deeply. From the way he stood, uncertain as to his footing, with constant fretful glances around, a flexing of his hand upon his staff, he appeared apprehensive. Though his eyes were mostly on Aude, he kept darting brief, worried glances at Bear and me.

Aude, barely looking up, finally said, "Goodman Piers, what brings you here?"

"Old dame," the man said with a hesitant, rocking motion that might have been a bow of courtesy but could just as well have been agitation, "Goodman William bade me come. His wife is heavy with child. Ready to burst. Being in great pain she's called for you to come without delay." He stole another glance at Bear, who was seated against one of the boulders. As for Troth, he seemed to take pains *not* to look at her. She pulled her hair across her mouth, hiding her disfigurement.

Only then did I realize it was something she had *stopped* doing for Bear and me.

"How fares the woman?" said Aude.

"Good dame, her labor is full of agony," the man cried. "She's frightened her babe is not set well."

Staring into the fire, Aude said, "Nerthus wants life. Aude will help." It was what she had said to me, when she first tended Bear.

The man wiped his mouth and the back of his neck with his hand. His eyes shifted nervously. Looking round at

Bear yet again, this time, he nodded. "Our Lord's peace to you, stranger," he murmured.

Bear said, "May all the grace of Our Blessed Lady be with your village woman."

"Aye, aye, exactly so," the man said with a vigorous nod. "May Jesus grant it." He seemed eased by Bear's Christian blessing. Then he added, "There were some men who passed through the village. They were looking for a large, red-bearded man. Perhaps you were the one."

Startled, I looked round to Bear.

"Who were they?" he asked.

"I know not."

Then Bear asked, "What came of them?"

"Since we knew nothing of you, they went away."

Aude reached out to Troth. The girl scurried over and with her help, the crone got to her feet. "The belt," she said, "the herbs."

Once ready, Aude said, "Come," to the girl and put one hand on her shoulder. The two moved toward the entryway.

"Old mother," Bear cried out. "God's blessings on you." Aude halted. She turned, and twisted round with her bird-like look to consider Bear and me with her one good eye. "Be blessed," she muttered.

An unhappy-looking Troth made a sign, which I under-stood to mean "Good-bye."

As soon as Aude and Troth went from the bower I turned to Bear. "Bear, you heard. Men are looking for you. We need to leave now."

Bear grunted. "God knows we have our enemies. But, Crispin, the man said they went off."

"The sooner we go, the safer."

He laughed. "The best time for elders to advise youth is when youth presumes to advise their elders."

"But I'm right!" I cried, now angry.

"Crispin, since those men had no way of knowing we were here, it's unlikely they'll come back. We're safest here. Anyway, by Saint Aldegon, I'm not strong enough to go. My fever lingers."

"You've not said so."

He shrugged. "A man's weakness is his best kept secret."

"Weakness is not your usual way of living."

"Crispin, I was close to *leaving* this living!"

"Has that so changed you?"

"Should it not?"

Feeling frustration and anger, I glared at him, then went to the entryway of the bower, and looked where Troth and Aude had gone. Then the thought came to me: if I'm ever truly to be free, I must act for myself. I turned back to Bear. "I'm going with them," I announced.

"Why?" he asked.

"I want to learn if anyone in the village is aware of us. We need to know how safe we are."

"You'll only draw attention."

"Bear, the man said only you were sought. Not me. Besides, you said you're not well. Then give way to me. I'm old enough."

He snorted. "The man who must prove himself a man is still a boy."

"Have you forgotten? You said I should feel free to disobey you at any time."

"Crispin!" I heard Bear cry. "Don't!"

But I had already started off.

13

 HEN I CAUGHT up with Aude and Troth, the girl acknowledged me with a glance of surprise. Aude paid no mind. She merely plodded on. No one spoke.

After perhaps two leagues, we began to move along a narrow track that suggested more frequent use. After another league, we came out of the woods and made our way into a shallow valley.

Some twelve or fifteen dwellings were scattered on either side of a muddy road with fields laid out in long strips, mostly in tillage. I took it to be Chaunton, the village of which Aude had spoken.

Houses were of timbered construction with wattle-and-daub walls and thatched roofs. A few had doors. No windows. Pigs, dogs, and geese roamed freely. I saw a small, decaying, gray stone church, its tower squat and square. The village sat well before it.

It was no different from other poor villages I had seen in my travels with Bear. Most likely it was owned—as Bear had once explained—by a distant lord or bishop or even an abbey, which saw nothing of the commune save rents or garnished goods.

No people were working the fields. Instead, a crowd was milling round the entryway of a house. I supposed it was where the birthing crisis was occurring. The number of people—perhaps twenty or twenty-five—gave me reason to think the whole town was there. From the custom of their dress, all appeared to be peasants, mostly men. But only women passed in and out of the house. As I knew from my own village, men were not allowed at a birth.

Our slow, awkward trudge into the village was soon noticed. All turned. A man detached himself from the others and began to run toward us, arms waving wildly. He was younger than the peasant who'd come to fetch us. His face was full of anguish.

"Dame Aude!" he cried. "Make haste! My wife's in mortal pain!" It was Goodman William.

Despite the plea, Aude made no alteration of her pace, but plodded on as before. Bent over as she was, I don't think she could have gone faster. Troth, meanwhile, pulled her hair across her face, hiding her disfigurement.

The peasant drew near. "Dame Aude," he shouted anew. "In the name of God's mercy, hurry!"

Aude, without looking up, mumbled, "Aude will try."

"Her pain is terrible," pressed the man as he drew close. "I fear she's in great danger. The bailiff is with her. "

Aude halted and peered up at the man. "The bailiff?" she said. "No man should be there."

"He claims the right!" said the man. With that he took hold of Aude, and pulled to make her move faster. "You need not fear: he knows you're coming," he went on. "He only insists there be none of your gods or magic."

Aude shook her head and tried—with little success—to resist the man's dragging hands. "Aude can only do as she does," she said.

Feeling awkward, out of place, suddenly not wishing to be associated with the two, I regretted I had come. I told myself I should go back to Bear. Even so, I stood there, wanting to see what would happen.

"But the girl," cried the man, darting an anxious look at Troth. "She mustn't come any closer."

Troth, keeping her gaze down, gripped Aude tighter.

"Why?" Aude demanded.

"God's mercy, woman!" cried the man. "You know the answer! She's Devil-marked. She'll bring peril to my wife. I beg you! In the name of Jesus, don't argue! Just hurry!"

Aude, with a vehement shake of her head, said, "Not without the girl."

The man tried to yank Troth away from Aude, but the girl clung to the old woman.

Though what I was witnessing upset me, I hardly knew what to do.

"You must hurry!" shouted the man at Aude. That time he pushed Troth back fiercely, enough to cause her pain. She turned to me with an open-faced appeal full of fright.

Unable to ignore Troth's plight, I jumped forward, and tried to pull Goodman William away from her. The man, taking notice of me for the first time, swung out with his fist, striking me on the shoulder with force enough to throw me off. He resumed his dragging of Aude.

Angry, I lunged and tried to pry William's hands away from Aude. Even as we thrashed about, a scream erupted from the house, a long, beseeching cry, full of awful anguish.

Ashen-faced, Goodman William released Aude and whirled toward the sound. Next moment, he swung back, went to his knees, clasped his hands, and looked up at Aude with eyes full of panic. "In God's mercy, woman!" he cried. "Help my wife!"

"I can only try," muttered the old dame, and moved forward again, clinging to Troth, as much as Troth clung to her.

As Aude drew near to the birthing house, the village folk retreated some paces. I could not tell if they moved from her because they did not wish to be near her, or to give her room. I was beyond their notice.

Then, just as Aude approached, the bailiff emerged from the house. At least I took him to be the bailiff. A big, burly man, he was dressed somewhat better than the others, with buskin boots and a paltry collar of some ragged sheep wool. His garments and hands were stained with blood.

When he appeared, the townspeople fell back to form a half circle behind him. Then, as Aude and Troth advanced, the bailiff stepped forward to block entry to the house.

"No," he shouted. "You must not go further! You're no Christian." It seemed to me his cry was as much to the townspeople as it was to her.

Aude halted. Small as she was, she seemed to diminish in size before this man.

But then the distraught husband tried to shove the bailiff away from the entry, crying, "She can save my wife!"

"Better she die than be damned," the bailiff said, refusing to move.

Another terrible cry came from the house.

It seemed to drive the husband mad. With a sudden leap, he wrapped his arms around the bailiff and dragged him away. "Go to her," he called to Aude. "I beg you! Go!"

Aude hesitated momentarily then went forward again. Troth stayed close. Next moment, the bailiff broke free from the husband and pounced at the old woman, only to miss. But he managed to take hold of Troth's arm. As the old woman went into the house, the bailiff yanked the girl back, forcing her to stay behind. As that happened, the husband followed Aude within and was also lost to my view.

The bailiff forcibly thrust Troth away from the house. "Evil thing!" he cried. "Begone!" He began to pummel her about her head and shoulders.

With sudden rage, Troth erupted. Whirling about, growling and grunting like some wild beast, she kicked and clawed at the bailiff. Small though she was, her attack came with such unexpected ferocity that the bailiff doubled over, putting his hands up to protect himself. The crowd, which had been inactive until then, came to life. With a shout, they rushed forward.

14

 T FIRST I thought the people were going to help Troth, and free her from the bailiff. It took just moments for me to realize otherwise: like a pack of attacking dogs, they joined the bailiff in beating Troth, kicking and clawing at her. "Kill

her. Kill the Devil-girl!" they screamed. Troth tried to resist but was quickly overwhelmed.

I was so stunned by what was happening, that at first I remained rooted where I was. But when I saw Troth fall I ran forward and dove among the swarm of brawling people. I struck out at whomever was before me, receiving as many blows—if not more—than I gave.

In the middle of this struggle came a long, drawn-out cry from the birthing house, a cry of appalling torment. It crested above all shouts and screams, enough to cause the mob to stay their fury.

In that brief lull, I wedged myself among the mob. Troth was cowering on the ground, crouched, arms up to protect her head, crying uncontrollably, bleeding. I put my arms round her, shouting, "Troth! It's me! Crispin!"

She gripped me.

Holding her tightly, I pushed back with my body, kicking and shoving as best I could, until I dragged the sobbing, gasping girl from beneath the frenzied swarm. The crowd did not even seem to know she was gone.

Once I'd freed Troth from the mob, I lifted her bodily and began to haul her away as best I could. But as we moved away, there came another shriek from the house: the tormented cry of the husband, Goodman William.

"Dead!" he screamed. "My wife and babe are dead!"

Hearing the death cry, the people as one shifted their attention to the house.

I stopped and turned, the weeping Troth still in my arms. As we looked on, Goodman William staggered out. Collapsing to his knees, head striking the earth, he beat the ground with his fists. "Dead! Dead!" he cried repeatedly.

The people went to him as if to provide comfort. As they did, the bailiff rushed into the house.

I let Troth down so that she stood on her own unsteady feet. She was trying to regain her breath, straining from me. Fearful that she'd go back and be caught by the crowd, I would not let her go.

Next moment, Aude appeared, blood upon her. She did not come on her own. The bailiff was dragging her by her hair. Being so light, so frail, the old woman could make but feeble resistance.

"Kill her!" shouted the bailiff, throwing her to the ground. "She worships foul gods! She caused the good wife's death!" He began to kick the fallen woman. Next moment, the people swarmed round and attacked Aude too. I could hear the blows, the cries.

Troth, with a horrific scream of pain—as though her heart were being ripped from her chest—struggled to free herself from me. Frightened that the villagers would turn on Troth, I clung to her tightly. Though she made dreadful, pleading sounds, I began to pull her away, fleeing as best I could.

At first I simply ran, paying no heed where I was going, save making my way out of the valley. No longer hearing cries from the village, I stopped and looked back. The crowd had drawn back. A mangled, bloody body lay before them. It was Aude.

I had no doubt that she was no longer alive.

Troth strained desperately to get away from me.

"There's no helping her," I said, unwilling to release her. "If you go back, they'll kill you, too."

Suddenly, Troth turned about and, sobbing uncontrollably, clutched me around my neck so tightly I gasped for breath.

"We need to get back to Bear," I told her. "I don't know the way. Troth, take us back to Bear."

I pried her grip loose, but kept holding her, fearful she would bolt back to Aude.

The two of us stared toward the village. The people had gathered round Aude's broken body. Then some one pointed in our direction. Two men started running toward us. One was the bailiff. I had little doubt what might happen.

"Troth," I pleaded, "we must get to Bear!"

Though weeping and struggling for breath, Troth bolted toward the forest following unseen paths. I, who but moments before was her protector, was now in need of her guidance.

15

E ARRIVED at the bower panting, gasping for breath. "Bear! Bear!" I cried as we burst in.

Troth, crying wildly, ran to Bear and buried her face in his chest. Taken by surprise, Bear wrapped his arms about her, even as he looked over at me for an explanation.

"They've killed Aude!" I shouted.

The blood seemed to drain from his face. "Who? Why?"

I told him what had happened as quickly as I could. "And they're coming after us," I said. "We must leave. Now!"

Bear looked at me then spoke into Troth's ear, loud enough for me to hear. "Troth, you can't stay here," he said. "You must come with us. We'll keep you safe."

Troth, her whole body shaking, as if the tumult of her emotions were writhing within, frantic to burst free, nodded mutely to Bear's words.

"Crispin," he called to me, "get whatever's ours. Hurry!"

I gathered up our sack, making sure it had our few things.

Gently, Bear pushed Troth away from him, and knelt before her, face to face.

I drew close, but didn't know what to do or say.

"Troth, hear me," Bear said. "By all that's holy, I swear by your gods and mine—by blessed Saint Bathild—we shall take care of you. Protect you. Do you understand me?"

Troth, sobbing, struggling for breath, and constantly smearing tears with dirty hands, looked around at me.

"We will, Troth, we will," I said, anxious that we leave.

Bear, not waiting for her to reply, asked, "Is there anything you wish to take?"

Crying with hard grief, she looked about, then ran out to the hawthorn tree and tore off a sprig, which she concealed among her clothing.

"Crispin," Bear called, "are you ready?"

I held up our sack. "I have everything."

Bear grasped the girl's hand. "We must go," he said.

Troth, as though unwilling to look at what she was leaving, pressed her face against Bear. He squeezed her close again.

I waited some few feet off.

Bear gazed upward toward the sun. He took a deep breath. "We'll go south," he said at last.

"Where?" I asked.

"I'm not sure," he replied. "Away."

With that Bear strode off, still holding on to the whimpering Troth. I came a few steps behind, sack in hand, looking back over my shoulder.

Suddenly Troth stopped. From her garments she took out the hawthorn, held it over her head, and murmured words I did not understand. Then, as though possessed, she turned and began to run.

16

S GOD WOULD HAVE IT, Troth led the way. We went southward, first running, then walking, then running again. My great fear was that Bear, not fully healed, would be unable to keep her pace. As it was, he had to pause and rest more than once. My own breathing was heavy. My legs ached.

Troth never looked back. Not once. All that she had been she seemed to put behind her. Backward glances were left to me. With all my fearful turnings I grew stiff-necked but saw nothing to suggest we were being followed.

I did not speak. But, then, I did not know what to say or what to think. In my thoughts I kept seeing what had happened. Its dreadfulness did not, would not fade. It brought on a constant shivering, as if death's cold hand gripped my neck and would not let it loose. What, I wondered, could Troth be seeing in *her* mind?

I recalled all the doubts I had about Aude and Troth: how I thought them evil, malignant spirits. Then—as if to excuse myself—I asked myself why my blessed God had *not* intervened in Aude's final moments. Why had *He* let it happen? Was He waiting for *me* to act? Was He unmoved because Aude worshipped other gods? I did not want to believe that of my most merciful Jesus. I also asked, what of Aude's gods, her beloved Nerthus? Why had *she* not saved Aude?

When my footsteps brought me no answers, I allowed myself the notion that to run away may well be the answer God provides.

It was dusk when we halted, still deep among the trees. How many leagues we had come, I could not begin to reckon. Troth, I think, could have gone on. It was Bear who insisted we must stop. Face flushed, in a filthy sweat, limping, he was exhausted.

Troth immediately sat down, rolled onto her stomach, and cradled her head in her arms, eyes turned from us. There she lay, unmoving, surely the most soul-weary of us all. Now and again she whimpered. Was this the first time she was so far from her bower? Away from Aude? I would have guessed as much.

"We better not light a fire," Bear cautioned.

"Do you think we've been pursued?"

"May God, in His mercy, say no. But it's best to take care."

"And food?" I said, realizing we had not brought any.

"We'll need to be content with nothing till the morrow," said Bear.

He sat next to Troth, close enough that she might know he was there. I sat on her other side, my knees drawn up, held by my arms.

The day faded to darkness. But if stars were above, I saw them not. Above us, tree leaves stirred as though to soothe the air. The footfalls of small creatures plucked the darkness. An owl hooted twice. Whether Troth slept, I could not tell. From the way Bear breathed I knew he was still awake.

"Bear," I called, "was it wrong for me to disobey you— when I went with Aude and Troth?"

"Wrong for you to have gone. Right that you were there."

"But . . . but one does not follow from the other."

"Ah, Crispin, you desire your freedom, don't you?"

"Yes . . . I do."

"Then best learn: freedom is not just to be, but to choose."

Though I tried to understand of what he meant, it was too hard. My thoughts drifted. "Bear," I asked, "what will happen to Troth?"

For a moment he said nothing. Then he said, "The girl's marked, unwanted. Feared. What's feared is abused. She'd perish. She must stay with us. Do you object?"

"No, no," I said in haste. "Not at all. But, Bear, where will we go?"

"To the southern coast, to the sea."

Remembering his words about the great ocean, something in me stirred. "And when we do . . ."

"It's easier to find employment in coastal towns. Men come and go. Perhaps, as well, men who've seen a bigger world have bigger hearts. Hopefully they'll be more accepting than peasant folk. We need some generosity. Let's pray to Saint Lufthildis that he'll protect us. He can be kind to those who are homeless."

"Are we homeless, then?"

"Perhaps all are," said Bear with a sigh. After some brooding silence he said, "When I was a child, there was a song often sung to me." Lifting his voice, he began to sing:

> Oh child, you are a pilgrim born in sin
> Who must forever wander in
> This world where death flies out
> of darkling doors
> To cast down Adam's kin,
> as he has done so oft before.
> For Adam, who, though once devout,
> In God's Eden of bright delight
> Caused eternal suffering throughout,
> By taking up the serpent's gift of
> never-ending night.

Then with a yawn, he said, "I'm exhausted. That running has heated my fever."

"Bear," I said, "will we never find some peace?"

"Every night," he murmured, "gives way to day."

"Does it *always* come?"

But Bear made no reply. I supposed he'd fallen asleep.

I—unable to get the images of Aude's slaying out of my head—could not sleep. I still felt wretched that *I* had once thought so badly of the crone, and of Troth.

"Blessed Saint Giles," I whispered, "it's hard to be a man." Full of remorse, I reached out and gently set my hand to Troth's back.

I did not know if she slept. Even so, I said: "Troth, in the name of my God, I beg your forgiveness for all my unworthy thoughts, and herewith make a sacred vow by my Sacred Mother that I will treat you with true kindness, that I will be a brother to you for all my days forever and anon."

To my surprise, she stirred, turned, and took my hand that had rested on her back, and set her broken mouth to it in a kiss. My heart swelled. I thought: though broken, a mouth cannot bestow such a forgiving blessing and be evil.

"Amen," I whispered to her.

She turned away. No more was said.

Greatly wearied, I made myself go on my knees and prayed desperately to my Saint Giles. I prayed for Aude's soul. I prayed too, for Troth's. I prayed, of course, for Bear.

By then I could hardly keep my eyes open. Even as I drifted off, I realized I'd yet to pray for my own keep. "Saint Giles!" I cried to the all-embracing night. "Help me have an open heart. Help me know my ignorance."

But mine was not an easy sleep. I had an ill-omened dream in which Aude's eyes—the blind one and the good—gazed at me from some distant place. In my troubled fancies

I knew she was seeing two futures, the good and the bad. Which future, I kept calling, would be mine?

And in my dream I heard Aude's mumbling voice. "Crispin," she was saying, "take heed. Be a man."

"Have I not saved Troth? What more need I do to become a man?" I cried.

The dream gave no answer.

17

E WOKE to a misty dawn. Like limp-winged moths emerging from cocoons, we tried to shrug out of our sleepiness. Once alert, we offered our prayers—I don't know if Troth made any—and then continued on, trudging beneath the crowded trees.

Troth went first, small, dressed in rags. Next came great Bear in his rough-made garment, without shoes, red beard unkempt, his two-pronged hat with bells a-jangle. I came last. I had my tunic, much torn. My hair had become long again. And filthy. On my back was our mostly empty sack.

An odd threesome we were!

By midmorning we reached the forest's edge. As if a veil

was being lifted, the bosky dimness melted. We stood upon a bluff and gazed upon unending rolling hills of new green, broken occasionally by clumps of leafy trees. Grass was thick and tall. Swallows swooped low before soaring up to distant heights. Beyond southern hills, the distant spire of a holy church pointed heavenward. Higher still was the sun, a pale white disk in the vast gray sky, a reminder of Aude's blind and milky eye.

"What is it about an empty countryside that seems so peaceful?" mused Bear.

"No people," I replied. "And we have been fleeing them for too long. Do you know where we are?"

Bear was taking his rest, sitting with his back against a tree, gazing out upon the open world. Close by, I leaned against another tree. Troth sat near Bear on the ground, clasping her knees in her arms, staring at the landscape. I wondered if she had ever seen so much land in one vista before.

That made me recall how much *I* had come to see of the world. Indeed, as I gazed out upon the unending land, I sensed how much more there was for me to see. The thought pleased me.

Bear glanced at the sun. "We are still going south," he said.

I asked, "Do you think anyone could be following us?"

Bear grunted. "There's an old saying: 'No matter where they go, the ignorant never travel far.'"

"May Heaven make it so," I said.

We sat and stared. After a while I said, "Forgive me, but I'm hungry."

"I am too," said Bear. "Troth, are you?"

She shook her head, but whether to give a yea or nay, it was hard to know.

"Then it's time we found some place to perform," said Bear. "That church," he said, pointing to the spire. "There should be a town or a village hard by. Crispin, it seems as if God wishes us to resume our old labors."

"Are you strong enough?" I asked.

"Methinks I must be," he returned.

"Will it be safe?"

"We can be watchful."

"And Troth?"

"In time, she needs to learn the drum, or make music in some other way. Or even dance. She can begin by passing around my cap for coins." He turned to her. "Troth," he said, "I suppose that with Aude not given to much talk, you had little reason to use words."

Troth nodded.

"Well, by Saint Ursula," said Bear, "we'll engage to teach you as much speech as we can until you converse as freely as a bishop. Come now, surely you can say your name."

Troth, alarm in her eyes, looked down, as if ashamed. She forced herself to look up again. Her hands were fists. Indeed, her face contorted with some inner struggle until she said, "Oth."

It was a reminder to me of her fierceness.

"Well done!" cried an exultant Bear, patting her back. "Did you hear, Crispin? Troth speaks her name as well as you and me." He added a private wink over her head so I would not contradict him. "By Saint Drogo, Troth, before long we shall have you giving speeches before King Edward at Westminster!

"Now, then, Troth, can you say *Crispin*? Can you say *Bear*?"

Shyly at first, the girl spoke her sounds with halting struggle. They were not the words as I might say them. But Bear was generous—as only he could be—in her praise. He would find no fault. And she, in her grave way, repeated the words over and again, determined to get them right.

Laughing with pleasure, Bear got up and took Troth by the hand so that she might walk by his side. We started for the place where the spire stood. As we went along, Bear paused to point out things and say them loudly to the girl, "Tree! Grass! Stone!" and such, insisting she repeat his words.

No matter what she uttered, Bear always told Troth she had spoken well, exceedingly well. I joined in the praise. The praise seemed to free her. She spoke with ever greater frequency.

From that point on, Troth spoke as if to make up for lost time. That it was hard for others to understand I can attest. And, God's truth, she never did speak much, or with great complexity. Indeed, I learned to read her hands and eyes as much as I heard her words. Those eyes of her spoke much. Bear and I, who heard her repeatedly, came to understand her manner, voice, and speech. Or, as Bear once said: "Mind, Crispin: a loving heart hears more than ears."

Thus when I render Troth's talk here on forward, I'll give it as we understood it, not the broken way it was spoke.

18

 S WE WENT on, Bear instructed Troth about our performances. "Now, Troth," he said, "Crispin and I shall show you how we

eke out pennies. We're heading for a village. Let's pray it's small and remote. When we arrive, Crispin will play the recorder while I sing, dance a jig, and juggle. If the good people look kindly upon us, we might earn enough to buy some bread."

I could see that, though Bear's words made Troth nervous, she made no response other than to nod.

Bear went on: "Therefore, Troth, you must study and learn from us, for in good time you must do your part. We'll have no sluggishness here. Have no fears. No harm will befall you. Just stay close to Crispin and me."

After going for perhaps a few leagues, we came upon a narrow road, which appeared sparsely used. Wagon tracks were shallow and for our brief passage we saw no one on it. It suggested an isolated place—just what we desired.

We pressed on, passing over a bridge that crossed a frothy stream. There we drank our fill. We also paused long enough for Bear to search out some smooth stones, which, by the way he hefted them, I guessed would be for his juggling. Then on we continued until the village we'd been seeking appeared before us.

Bear handed me the recorder.

"There, you see?" he said, as I gave a few fluttering trills. "We're as ripe and reedy as ever."

"Are you?" I asked, doubting it.

"Crispin," he said, "I think we have no choice." He flexed his arms and hands until his knuckles cracked, smoothed his beard and took a deep breath.

Excited to reengage with our old life, I put the recorder to my lips and offered up a light and lilting air, an easy one to step. Bear slipped into it, like foot to boot, and began his dance.

To see Bear romp caused Troth's eyes to open wide with delight, for—fever or no—Bear was stepping high and lively, now moving forward, heading for the town, hat bells a-jingle. Step for step I was with him with all my being, piping out my pithy tune.

Troth ran to keep up with us, calling, "Bear! Crispin! Wait for me!"

As God willed, it was a miserably poor village we'd come to. But then, the kingdom had no end to such impoverishment. Hardly bigger than Chaunton, it was far less than my Stromford. Otherwise, it was much the same and thus unworthy of description. No doubt it was smaller than its name, which no one ever bothered to divulge. Perhaps it had none.

As always, the children were the first to see us come. Where they came from one never knew, but come they did, running and tumbling like tail-shaking, squealing piglets at their play. No doubt we were as rare as furry eggs. They laughed and clapped their hands. Some made attempts to dance like Bear, skipping along, knees high, and hands clapping, as we came into what passed for the center of the village.

I think Bear loved these parades of tumbling, gleeful youth as he headed—in our normal fashion—for the church.

The village church proved fairly large and suggested that the community it served had once been larger, perhaps before the great sickness. I could see Troth eyeing the building with wonder. Remembering tiny Chaunton, no doubt it was the biggest structure she had ever seen. It allowed me to think that I had seen much of the world.

When we drew close to the church porch, Bear sank to his knees and removed his cap with a generous flourish, making the bells ring with merriment.

I stopped playing and knelt by his side, head bowed. Troth, imitating us, did the same, staying close to me. She was tense, with eyes for everything, while trying to shield her mouth with her hair. I reached out and tried to reassure her with a touch. She edged nearer.

As curious villagers gathered round we kept in place. It was not long before a priest arrived. He was an elderly, tonsured man, tall and thin, who looked—despite his advanced age—strong as an ox. Indeed, it appeared as if he had just come in from the fields, and had been working hard.

"My blessings on you, strangers," called the priest, as he approached. "Do you wish words with me?"

Bear gave his usual response, with just enough alterations to make it appear fresh upon his lips: "Most reverend Father," he began, head still bowed, but loud enough so all might hear, "I, known as Bear, am a juggler. My son, daughter, and I, being but lowly pilgrims, are making our way from York City toward Canterbury to pay our humble homage to England's sainted Becket, there to beseech his blessings upon the children's late deceased mother, my lawful, churched wife. For so doing we humbly ask your approval."

I noted that Bear now included Troth as his daughter, as well as providing us with a common mother and him a wife. I wondered if Troth had heard and what would be her thoughts.

"You may gladly have my blessing," returned the priest, and he lifted his hand to bless us with his Latin words and the sign of the cross. "But I suspect," he added with a generous smile, "there's something else you wish."

"My children and I," Bear went on, "beg leave to perform some simple songs and dances for the greater glory of God, for this fair village, and for his grace, King Edward, England's golden lion, with whom I have had the honor of fighting on the victorious fields of France."

"With King Edward, you say?" said the priest.

"Himself."

"Did you not know he has died?"

"Died!" cried Bear, looking up sharply. "When?"

"The news reached us these past few days."

"And is Edward's son, the Duke of Lancaster, the new king?" asked Bear.

"Apparently not. It's the true heir, the late king's grandson, Richard of Bordeaux, who has been crowned. God grant him long life! But mark this: it seems that when our young king was crowned—he's been styled Richard the Second—and was being carried away, one of his shoes fell off. An ill prophecy for his reign."

"Who put it back on?"

"His uncle, the duke. Still, let's pray there'll be some measure of peace for a while. God knows, despite the truce, the word is the war in France goes on."

"How far are we from the coast?" Bear inquired.

"The sea?" returned the priest. "The closest port is the town of Rye. Perhaps a week's journey. I've never seen it myself, but there are those among us who can tell you the way."

"Father," said Bear, "I'm grateful for your information and your blessing." That said, he sprang up and with a nod to me—his signal for me to start—and I commenced to play and Bear to dance.

As God was kind to us, we earned enough to purchase three loaves of bread. Bear, I could see, was much wearied. But no one spoke ill—to our hearing—of Troth, who had shyly passed Bear's hat.

That night we were allowed to sleep in a donkey stall, sharing our place with the beast. The cost to us was another song and dance for the crofter's family. Still, this man not only provided us a place to sleep, but some rare mutton and turnip and enough to drink.

"Bear," I asked as we sat about after eating, "will the king's death make a difference to us?"

Troth looked up. "What's . . . king?" she asked.

To which Bear replied: "A king, Troth, is the ruler our loving God bestows upon us. While at times the gift appears to bless us, at other times it seems meant as a trial."

"Is the new one good or bad?" I asked.

"He's a child. Some nine years old."

"Nine!" I cried.

"And whereas an infant may still have angels hovering round his head, as king he'll more likely bring on the Devil. The point being, he'll not truly reign. Not for years. It will be his uncle who holds the power, if not the scepter."

"Who is that?"

"The Duke of Lancaster, John of Ghent."

"The one who replaced the king's shoe?" asked Troth.

"Exactly so. And small events can foretell great acts. There are four things that can be said for the Duke: He's brother to the late king. The wealthiest man in all England. Perhaps the world. England's most powerful man. And the most hated."

"Why hated?" I asked.

"He's haughty. A poor soldier. A man greedy for power."

No one spoke for a while. Not until a somber Troth stood before Bear and said, "Bear . . . am I . . . your daughter now?"

Bear's somber mood was replaced by a grin. He clapped a large hand on my shoulder, another on hers. "If this lad can be my son," he said, "you can be my daughter. Will you have me?"

To this the ever-solemn Troth said, "I will."

To which I said, "Then, Troth, I am your brother."

"So be it!" cried Bear, and reaching out with his great

arms he encircled and bussed us both. "My two cubs!" He laughed.

Was ever a family more wondrously made?

19

E PRESSED ON in a southerly direction, Bear choosing not to travel by any road. It took us longer, but I suspected he picked a leisurely pace, the more to mend. In truth he was in grim humor, not given to much jesting or even speaking. While he did not say, I suppose he also thought Troth would be better off with just us. For her part, she remained mostly mute, but always close. I was pleased that there were just the three of us.

The first night after our visit to the small village, we stopped in a clump of small trees near the top of a hill. For food, we ate some bread and cheese we had purchased.

"What will we find in that place called Rye?" I asked.

"I've never been," he said. "I know it only as a port."

"Is it safe there?"

He shrugged. "As always, we must watch, listen, and beyond all else, pray."

"To whom?"

"Whoever hears you best."

"Bear," I asked, "why are there so many saints?"

"I suppose," said Bear, "this wretched world has so many woes, even God almighty needs help."

Indeed, that night he chose to drill us—both Troth and me—in using a pike (a tree branch) and a dagger (a stick) to defend ourselves.

"Do you think we're being followed?" Troth asked.

"Alas," he said, "we all have our enemies. A soldier I once knew used to say, 'He who thinks his enemies are fools is the bigger fool.'"

Avoiding villages for a few days, we continued south. To pass the time I tried to get Bear to talk about some of the places he had visited.

Once I said, "Tell us what your soldiering days were like."

He shook his great head. "I'd rather not talk of those things."

"Why?" I demanded.

"Some things are too awful to want a second seeing."

"You're only telling."

"A good telling is a good seeing," he returned. "And it was war."

"What is *war*?" asked Troth.

"Dear Troth, may God grant it never touches you," said a grim-faced Bear.

"Then tell us," I said, "about that place you *never* saw—the one which has no kings, armies or wars—that land of ice."

"Iceland?" he said, with a broad grin. "I don't even know if it exists."

"Then," I suggested, "you can make it even better."

"I suppose—from its name—it's all ice." That said, he spun some marvelous tales—stories of giants, of trolls and dragons, of great deeds by ice-draped warriors.

Troth and I listened, enthralled.

To earn our necessary bread we performed three times, always heading south. Though these villages were pitiful places, we gathered enough thin coins to eat.

The second time we performed, Troth joined in on her own. Taking Bear's hat, she shook it rhythmically, adding to our sound. What pleased her most, I think, was that few paid her any mind. All eyes were set on Bear, his dancing and juggling.

By night, Bear told us more fabulous tales, of holy saints and their miracles, of beasts and the great acts of the ancients. It was as if we traveled more by night—

not moving, just listening—than we did all day by foot.

Those were nights of joy: the cloaking darkness our guardian, the spread of stars above, each star a promise of God's infinite grace, a blessed eye upon our little family. Oh, how I adored that feeling of *us*, the embrace of star-blessed love! If we could have been that way forever—a family below that overarching heaven which flowed on so gracefully—I would have been much content.

But as we pressed on I began to notice something: when we were in the villages to perform, Bear made a point of going off to speak alone to some of the menfolk. It was as he'd done before in Great Wexly—though at the time I did not know it—when he was gathering information for John Ball's brotherhood. Now, when he did this, he seemed glum, and as we moved farther south, increasingly so.

"Is it news about the new king you're seeking?" I asked when he came back one such time.

"There is no news of him," was his curt reply.

"Are you hearing word of the brotherhood, then?"

He made a face. "Let's pray we never see their like again."

"But something is troubling you," I persisted.

"We shall have to see," was all the answer he allowed.

Avoiding common roads, and, for a time, even villages, we approached the port of Rye from the north. Thus we followed footpaths of which there were increasing numbers, often wending our way through grazing flocks of bleating sheep.

As it fell out, long before the town came into sight, I began to smell something I never had before. It was strong, and fairly reeked of I knew not what.

"What is *that*?" I demanded of Bear, for it made my nose itch.

"You're smelling the sea," he said.

"What's *sea*?" asked Troth.

Bear looked to me.

"The sea, Troth," I replied with much self-assurance, "is water—also called ocean—and it covers the earth more than land." That said, both Troth and I looked to Bear: I to see if I'd spoken correctly; Troth, I suspect, in disbelief.

"Crispin speaks true," said a grinning Bear to both of us.

Excited to see something so vast and strange as *sea*, I urged us on, and soon enough, as we came round a stand of trees, the town we had been seeking lay before us.

And then I learned what was worrying Bear.

20

HE ANCIENT TOWN of Rye is situated on a high knob of land like a clenched fist. It is surrounded on three sides by low water channels, rivers, and a marshy mix of sand and sea. These waters flow directly into a bay, the bay opening to the sea, though coming from the north as we did, the sea was hidden by the rise of land.

But Rye itself, being elevated, could be observed from a distance. There was a large cluster of houses and a tower that looked to be a castle. A church spire could also be seen. What we also saw was a large amount of hazy smoke.

"The town. It's on fire!" I said, proclaiming the obvious.

"Then it's true," he said.

"What's true?" I demanded.

"I was told French and Castilians attacked and laid waste to Rye. I didn't wish to believe them."

"Why not?"

He shook his great head. "You heard the priest: there's supposed to be a truce in the war. An attack at this time seemed unlikely. But it's true."

"Who told you about it?"

"In the towns—some of the people shared the news."

"Why would Rye be attacked?" I asked.

"When England claimed the French crown, we brought the war to them. They've now returned the compliment."

"Is that the meaning of the new king's lost shoe? The omen that priest spoke of?"

"Or," said Bear, "the French wishing to test the young king."

"Bear . . . are they still here?"

"I was told they struck hard and fast, and fled. It should be safe. Let's hope so."

To reach the town we had to cross one of the rivers, which was so wide we had to pay a ferryman one of our well-worn pennies to pole us across.

He was an old man, stooped and grizzled, whose skin was as dark and speckled as a brown egg, his boat a narrow hollowed-out log with a bottom as flat as any shoe. At first I feared we might tumble into the water, but the man showed his skill and kept us on even keel.

"Tell us of the attack," Bear said to this man as he carried us to the other shore.

"It was a sweet, cloudless day when they came," was the reply. "They came by sea, at dawn, swooping in, killing almost seventy. Four men were taken away for ransom. Looting was rampant. Many homes were burned. They burnt our church, stealing everything they could, even taking the bells." He paused in his poling to lift a fist in anger. "May God strike them down, hard!" He marked his words with a shove upon his pole, punctuating them by spitting into the water.

"And they claim Saint Dennis as their protector, he who is a defense against strife. May Jesus blast them all."

"Was there no resistance?" asked Bear.

"We did resist. Fiercely. But were ill-prepared. Those who failed in their responsibility have paid the penalty."

"How so?" asked Bear.

"Execution," said the man. "God rot them." He spat into the water.

"That," suggested Bear, "will surely make them better prepared next time."

The man went on: "Happily after two days, the abbot of St. Martin's—his name is Hamo—led a force to drive them away."

"And all this took place—when?" asked Bear.

"Seven days ago," said the man. "And with news of the

sacking, the traders have shied away. But perhaps some—not knowing of our plight—will yet arrive. Was there somewhere you wished to sail?"

"Not us," Bear said.

"You're strangers. Where do you come from?"

"York," said Bear, who had clearly been prepared for this question.

"Did they attack elsewhere?"

"We don't know," said Bear. "We have been traveling."

"Then travel on to France or Castile and slay them all for me," said the man, who, with a final shove, beached the little boat upon a shingle of gravel and sand.

On the shore, heaps of burnt and half-burnt wood lay about at random, no doubt dragged there to rot. They stank mightily. Whatever docking or lifting machines had existed, were destroyed. It was also there that I first saw a cog, the sort of boat Bear told me about, that carried most goods to other ports.

Above us stood the town of Rye, situated on a hill behind the town's portal called the Landgate. The gate itself had escaped destruction.

Once we entered Rye's grid of streets, we lost the rich tang of sea, to be enveloped by the stench of the town, the normal stink of offal, ordure, and slops. There was also the reek of destruction. Many a house had been burnt, with a fair number still smoking. Most houses were without roofs, mullioned windows destroyed, shutters aslant. Indeed, no wood structure was left unharmed. Charred wood was so common that the acrid smell of burn and smoke stuffed our noses. Everywhere was the chaos of destruction: the litter of countless broken things, clay, cloth, and wood. Stone structures fared somewhat better.

In two places we saw the charred and stinking bodies of fly-encrusted dogs, and even, to my horror, a foul human not yet claimed.

Hardly a wonder, then, that the survivors paid scant attention to us. The people of Rye moved slowly, faces taut with bewilderment and suffering. Some must have been in great pain, for they were bandaged, or limped, showing hurt in many ways. For others, the grief must have been contained within. When children looked at us, they did so furtively, clinging to their elders' legs.

"Why did the French do this?" asked Troth.

"We did the same to them," returned Bear quietly. He seemed much disturbed.

The town being on a hill, we trudged upward along its narrow, winding streets, toward the top. No rumble and uproar of people as in Great Wexly. No flashes of joy as we had seen in even smaller towns. No chatter or light laughter such as one normally hears. Here, only destruction to see and terror to sense, broken now and again by the thud of what must have been hammers attempting to set things aright—or perhaps in making coffins.

At the town's crown we came to Rye's church—or what had become of the church. Doors had been wrenched away. Windows were broken. Shards of colored glass lay about on the ground—as if a rainbow had fallen from the sky and shattered.

When we looked within, all was smashed, much of it buried beneath the mangled remains of a collapsed and still-smoldering roof.

"Was it the infidels who did this?" I asked, shocked by the desecration of such a holy place.

"There are no infidels in France," said a grim Bear, as he turned away. "Just Christians. Like me."

We went forward and there I had my first look upon the great sea.

What I saw astounded me: a vast plain of flat and endlessly empty gray, which was overwhelming. The word *forever* was thus made real, the boundaries of my world turned infinite.

Thus it was that in one brief time I saw the hand of

God's creation as thrice awesome—and the hand of man's destruction, frightening three times more.

21

HAT NIGHT, Bear found us a place in an inn. At least what remained of one. Like the rest of Rye it was much despoiled, though the innkeeper—a woman named Benedicta—and her son Luke were laboring hard to rebuild. The inn bore the name of Michael the Archangel—the one who can protect mariners against storms. A charred sign displayed his symbol: a dragon with a sword.

Half the inn's roof was gone. Stone walls, by God's mercy, were mostly intact though dressed in soot. Doors were broken. Most of the wine and ale pillaged. The same for victuals.

Worst of all, Benedicta, a widow woman, had one of her two sons slain by the marauding troops. A tall, stately woman, with long black hair in a single braid and black garments, she was severe-looking in her sorrow. There being little custom since the attack, she was willing to have us and our paltry pennies. Despite her great grief, she welcomed us as ones who had no such loss as she, so she could open her sorrow to Bear, who always served as a broad funnel for people's grief. With so many of her neighbors consumed by loss, the poor woman could find no pity, and she was in sore need of some.

She set a broken table for us, and somehow secured trenchers and some small meat with not enough rot to keep us off. Then she and her surviving son—twice my age and a likeness of his mother—joined us, and talked of their heartache to Bear. In so doing, they struck a friendship. Bear told her that Troth and I were his children and he a widower.

While they talked, Troth and I stayed in a quiet corner and listened. After much discussion of the attack, they spoke of the late King Edward, of Richard the new boy king, the Duke of Lancaster, and the war with France, which had gone so poorly for England of late.

Much land—and many men—had been lost in the Aquitaine, which is where Benedicta's husband had died two years previous. A truce had been made between England and France, but she said English soldiers had been abandoned in France and they fought on as brigands.

The woman asked Bear to tell his story. Perhaps to gain

her empathy, he revealed that he, too, had been a soldier and spoke of fighting in France with the Black Prince. "It was hard and terrible," he told her.

She asked Bear if he knew her husband, and named the knight with whom he fought.

Bear shook his head. "There were too many."

"Now you must tell me why are you here," said Benedicta. "Or do you mean to enlist again?"

"Not I!" cried Bear with alacrity. "We're only wandering minstrels, hoping to stay awhile."

"I fear you won't earn much with your music and dancing here," she said. "People will cling to what they have."

Seeing Bear downcast, the woman said, "What say you labor for me in return for food and lodging? I need the help."

"I've not my usual strength," said Bear.

"I'm sure it's enough."

A bargain was quickly made.

Thus commenced a pleasing, even restful time as we stayed on at the broken inn. With a loan from Benedicta, Bear was able to purchase new clothing—breeches, shift, hose—and, at last, some boots. Troth was also garbed, though she refused wimple on her head and shoes. It was appealing to see her mix of solemn pleasure and discomfort in new clothing, a bird with new plumage, though her plumage was but a simple wool kirtle.

For work, Bear was called upon for lifting, hauling, and repairing. While he was not as strong as he had been, he was strong enough. I prayed he'd regain it all.

Indeed, concerned for his state, I kept a self-appointed task of being his—and Troth's—protector. At times I thought we should go elsewhere, to one of the lands Bear had spoken of, so as to be free of all thoughts of pursuit.

Of this, however, I said nothing, knowing my restlessness was stirred not just by fear, but also by seeing the ships and sea, feeling their allure. For I, who had lived so confined, so closed, saw the sea as boundary-free, a notion I found exciting.

Meanwhile, Troth and I were asked to do smaller tasks—to clean or fetch. She was too shy to talk to others. Only with me would she chatter. Thus she and I, finding more time to be alone, learned more about one another's lives.

She was much taken by the story of my mother's secret life, how I had fled my town, my meeting with Bear, and what happened in Great Wexly. For my part, I was held by her tales of life with Aude in the forest.

In truth, just as I had come to think of myself as insep-arable from Bear, I now felt much the same for Troth.

Once she suddenly said to me: "Crispin, when you first saw me did you think me very strange?"

I gazed at her, and realized that I considered her differ-ently from how I had at first. Then I surely saw the disfig-urement. Now I saw—Troth. Still, I wondered how she wanted me to answer, but quickly decided she would trust me only if I told her true.

"Did I think you strange?" I echoed. "Yes."

"Why?"

"You were different. The way you lived."

"My mouth?"

"That too."

"And now?" she asked, gazing at me with eyes that welled with tears.

I reached out and placed my hand on her cheek. "Next to Bear . . ." I stammered, "I have no better friend."

She smeared the tears from her face then took from her kirtle the sprig of hawthorn she had carried from the forest.

"Why did you take that?" I asked.

"Aude would bless me beneath that tree. She told me a twig of it would bind me to the ones I love."

"Then the magic works," I said.

She threw herself at me, hugged me and wept while I stroked her tangled hair.

Once she suddenly said to me, "Bear has a secret sorrow."

"How do you know?"

"I see it in him," she said.

"I think you're right," I agreed. "At times he's almost told me. But I didn't want to hear."

"Why?"

"I don't want to think any less of him. Do you know what troubles him?"

"Something he regrets."

"How do you know that?"

"I see it."

"Is it very bad?"

"He thinks so."

I sighed. I said, "Someday I will get him to talk about it."

When I had a chance, I took to wandering about Rye alone. It was not that I did not wish to be with Bear or Troth, but I enjoyed my freedom.

Rye was not nearly as big as Great Wexly, and its state of devastation had reduced it further. The very smallness of the town allowed me to see the whole of it, to find my way with increasing ease.

The rubble from the attacks was slowly being cleared. Repairs were being made. Houses were starting to be rebuilt. Even the church began to be cleaned. There was talk of a town wall for defense.

And for the first time, I came to meet with other boys. In my village of Stromford, more often than not I was shunned. It was rare for anyone to befriend me. In Rye, the boys knew nothing of me, save what they saw. Echoing Bear, I claimed York as my home, and that I was traveling with my father and sister as a performing minstrel.

Not knowing what to expect, at first I was uneasy, but the boys took me at my word—the more so as I often helped them in their labors. What's more, they envied my juggling. On my part, I took great pleasure in being with them.

Some had been on ships and had traveled to distant places. Others were apprentices learning trades: bakers, masons, and others. Others complained of hard masters and harsh parents, while some had only words of kindness for the same.

All had tales of the attack, speaking with bitter anger of the killing, looting, and cruelty. Family losses were great and awful to hear. Many swore revenge upon the French and Castilians.

But despite their doleful recollections, sweetest to me

was their irrepressible, raucous sense of life; their boisterous, braggart ways. Despite their losses, these boys found ways to joke and tease among themselves and did the same to me. To be among them made me feel older, wiser, smarter. I was keen to learn. To have what are called friends, to have boys my age greet me by my true name—with pleasure—was a whole new joy for me.

I even made a particular friend, Geoffrey by name, whose father was a mariner. Geoffrey told me many tales about ships and the sea. Once he confided—bragging I would say—that his father had served on a brigand ship attacking French ports.

Not to be outdone, I told him that *my* father—Bear— had been in a secret brotherhood, but having left it, we needed to be on the watch for them. Such secrets sealed our friendship.

One day Geoffrey took me in a little boat and we went out onto the waters. How amazing to float, to see the land from offshore. When he let me cast a line I caught a fish. As I hauled it in, I could not keep from laughing with delight. That night, Benedicta cooked it and it was fine. My being swelled with pleasure.

I did not let a day pass—sometimes with Geoffrey, sometimes alone, sometimes with Troth—without looking to see what ships had come in. As I learned, before the French and Castilian attack, many vessels had come. Now, though fewer, enough arrived for me to study them.

There were smaller boats used by fisher folk. And once I saw a huge hulc. But the ships that drew me most—perhaps because of their colorful sails and mariners speaking so many tongues—were the cogs, which were the seagoing horses of the coastal fleet.

These cogs were some seventy-five feet in length, twenty-five at the widest. They were built of huge beams with smaller overlapping boards—"clinkered," as it was called—for a hull. A single tall mast—thick and forty feet in height—set somewhat forward of midship, bore a cross spar from which hung a great, square canvas sail. Rough oak planking made for a deck.

The front of the boat—they called it a bow—was sharp and poked up. The rear of the boat was higher and called a "castle." At the castle's highest point was a great steering oar—a rudder they named it—so heavy it took a strong man to shift it.

A cog could carry all manner of goods, mostly in barrels—they called them tuns—for trade. They carried people, sometimes soldiers and horses. The attacking soldiers had come in cogs.

Not only did the ships hold my fascination, they fed my fancy of becoming a mariner.

One evening Benedicta told us about the death of her husband in France. "It was at a siege," she said. "Or so I was told. I don't know where. Nor how."

Bear said he had taken part in more than one such siege, which was something I had not heard before. "For the most part they can be tedious," he said. "But then they turn brutal."

"Like the French?" asked Benedicta's son.

At a loss for words, Bear ruffled his beard and shook his head. "I don't like to say."

The room was filled with a painful silence, after which Bear stood up and left the room.

Later that night, when I realized Bear had not come to sleep, I went outside. Bear was sitting with his back to a wall, staring up at the star-filled sky.

"Is something wrong?" I said.

"No," he said curtly.

"Bear," I said, "why don't you say what happened when you were a soldier?"

He did not respond.

"Why won't you tell me?" I asked.

At first he did not speak. Then he said, "It is hard to tell myself."

"What do you mean?"

"Crispin, war is another world. To be a soldier is to be another person." He was breathing painfully, as if it were hard to speak. "I sinned much. In my heart I cannot even ask forgiveness for what should not be forgiven. I can only pray that my Lord will have mercy on me."

"What did you *do*?" I asked, much troubled.

"Go to sleep, Crispin," he said with weary irritation. "I don't wish to speak of it."

I returned to the room where we slept. As I lay down I heard Troth say, "Crispin, is something the matter?"

"I don't know," I said, and told her of my conversation. After she had listened, Troth said, "Aude used to say there are places *in* people we can't see. But they are there."

I thought for a while and then I whispered, "Troth, once, when Bear was ill he talked about a chained bear that was kept in captivity—as if the links of the chain were his sins. He told me he took his name from that bear. And another time he said, 'To love a man, you must know his sins.'"

"Crispin," she said, "you know Bear. You know he's good."

Lying there in the darkness, I thought: is that what it is to be older—to know there are things you are afraid to know?

HILE BEAR WORKED at the inn with Luke, Troth and I spent much time together. We often wandered about Rye, looking upon its world.

Troth was like a chest that had become unlocked. There was so much she wished to know. For her, Rye was a vast place full of new things. I marveled at what she noticed, wondered, and asked about. Though I wanted to appear knowledgeable, I could not always supply answers. "Ask Bear," I often had to say.

As we wandered, there were times Troth hid her face—for people would stare, point, and even call her names—which made her shy. She was never so with me. My friends soon accepted her.

In the evenings, back with Bear, who talked expansively to Benedicta and Luke, Troth and I found in exchanged glances all the talk we needed. Sometimes we communicated with the hand signs that had become our secret language.

I talked freely to Bear—or at least tried to—but since

that time when he would *not* talk, I was much aware there were things in him he did not want me to know. It grieved me to see how he had changed: no longer the boisterous believer in his own bigness, when even his rebukes made one smile, when his jests taunted all, when his very being could embrace the whole world.

But when Troth and I talked, we were equals. I could say anything to her, and she to me.

"If God could give you what you most wished," I once asked her, "what would it be?"

"Aude."

"And if not her?"

"To be with Bear . . . and you," she replied.

After a moment she asked me the same question, and I replied, "To be with Bear and you."

"Then it's the same prayer," she said, "and therefore perhaps the stronger."

Then I asked, "If you could *be* anything you desired, what would it be?"

She replied: "Ordinary. And you?" she asked.

"A man."

"Like Bear?"

I was about to give a quick *yes*, for I did so admire and love him. But I found myself hesitating and unsure of my words, except to think, I was not him. I must be myself, Crispin.

"No," I said quietly, cautious to speak so. "I think . . . I want to be different. Perhaps a mariner."

So it was that as often as I could, I took her to look upon the sea, sitting on the high bluff near the large castle tower that survived the attack. Most often we sat in silence and did little more than stare upon the sea's great expanse.

Once she asked, "Crispin, what lies beyond the sea?" She was pointing to the farthest line of ocean—where water and sky met.

"In faith, I don't know."

"Is there *anything*? Or *is* that the edge of the world?"

"I suppose what you can't see," I replied, "is always the edge. And fearsome to look over."

"Aude often spoke of the edge of the world." Then she said, "Could it be Nerthus's world?"

"Which is?"

"The land *beyond*. Where . . . I hope Aude is. Crispin, shall we stay in Rye?"

"I want to be free to see the world."

"Even to the edge?"

"Aye."

She said, "I'd go with you."

"I would like that."

It was some twenty days or so after we arrived, on a late afternoon, the dark already descending, when Benedicta sent me to the miller for some flour. As I was wont to do, I took the long way about to the highest point, near the castle, so I could look upon the sunset sea which I found endlessly beguiling.

"Crispin!" I heard.

Taken by surprise, I turned. It was my friend Geoffrey, who had run up. "I've been looking everywhere for you!" he called. His face was flushed.

"Is something the matter?"

"That brotherhood," he burst out.

"What do you mean?"

"You told me your father was being pursued by some brotherhood. Three men have come to town. They have been asking for your father."

I thanked him then fled back to the inn and found Bear, Benedicta, and Luke hauling a beam upon their shoulders. Fearful of speaking too openly, I ran to find Troth. She was in the courtyard, sweeping with an old straw broom.

"Troth!" I cried, "they've come."

She turned pale. "The men from Chaunton?" she cried.

"No, ones seeking Bear. You must gather our things."

She dropped her broom and followed as I ran back to Bear. In the interval the beam had been set it its proper place.

"Bear," I said. "I must speak with you."

"You're free to do so."

"I . . . I think it best," I stammered, "that it's only for your ears."

"Come now, we have no secrets from our friends."

I looked from him to the innkeeper. Deciding there was no time to argue, I blurted out, "They've come."

"Who's come?" said Benedicta.

"Ball's brotherhood."

Bear's face stiffened. "How do you know?"

"A friend told me three men have come to town and were asking for you. I did not see them"

"Sins of Satan!" Bear swore. He slumped against the wall, defeat in his face. It was shocking for me to see him so, but it confirmed what we had to do. "I was hoping it would be otherwise."

"Bear," I said, "we *must* leave."

He shook his head. "Crispin, they would only follow," he said.

"We can take a boat," I said. "Sail away from England. Go to one of those places of which you spoke."

Bear bowed his head. "Let them come, Crispin. We'll be done with them."

He looked up at me with weary eyes. To my dismay I saw him willing to accept defeat. "Bear," I pleaded, struggling to find a way to move him, "there are three of them. If you can't fight them off, what would become of me? And Troth?"

That touched him. He looked at Benedicta, as if he was asking her.

"Rye is a small place," she said. "It will take only a short time before you're pointed out. Crispin's right. You best go."

"There are two cogs on the quay," I quickly said.

Bear turned to me. "How do you know?"

"I look every day."

Bear studied his hands as if to measure their strength. Then once again he turned to the innkeeper.

"When it is safe," she whispered, "you can return. I'll be here."

Bear took in a great breath. "God grant it. Very well. Crispin, gather our things."

"Troth has them," I replied.

Benedicta turned to Luke. "Go with him," she said. "I'll stay here, and deal if necessary."

"Can you?" asked Bear.

"As God knows, there's little fear left in me."

She and Bear embraced one another. As we were leaving, the innkeeper handed Bear some coins and a bullock dagger. "Trust in God and this."

"Can you spare it?" asked Bear.

"I can." She turned back to Luke. "Take them down and around the western cliff," the innkeeper advised. "Are you sure there were cogs?" she asked me.

I nodded.

"Make sure you bring them to the one that's leaving soonest," she said to her son.

Luke nodded his understanding. For a moment Bear and Benedicta gazed at one another. There was great sadness in their faces.

"Bear," I cried, "we must go!"

Thus we quit the inn, all but running.

23

 HE SOUTHERN CLIFF that fronted Rye was rocky and steep, but more steplike than not, so that we could climb down with

ease. Moreover, Luke knew a path that in the growing darkness we would never have found on our own. With him going first, followed by Bear, Troth, and finally me, it took moments for us to reach the rocky base.

"Keep close," Bear whispered.

Going as quickly as we could, we picked our way over boulders and stones until we turned the bend of Rye's bluff. Coming round we saw a large fire burning on the beach. By the gleaming firelight, I saw the two cogs I had seen earlier. They had been hauled up on the beach.

I looked to Bear. "There, you see."

"We can but try," he said and turned to Luke. "We'd best go on alone. Your mother may need you. In any case, if we can't leave by boat, we'll leave by another way. I'll send word. Many blessings on your kindness."

Luke had no desire to linger. "God give you grace," he said and hastened away, running back the way we'd come.

As soon as he left, we three continued along the beach. Drawing closer, we could see that while there were two cogs, just one had people about—four in number. By the light of the fire we could see they were brawny fellows, working in pairs to load a host of barrels. Once the barrels were on the ship they wrestled them down a hatch to the hold. On the beach were some sixteen more tuns.

"Keep a look about," Bear warned.

That said, we advanced upon the cog.

"God mend all," called Bear as he approached. Troth and I held back some steps.

The men paused in their work. Once they saw who we were, they went on with their labor.

"Might I speak to the ship's master?" asked Bear.

One of the men standing on the beach, who was just bringing a barrel forward, called out. "I'm here."

He was a squat, bulky man, whose flat, weathered face featured bulging eyes, a high forehead, and small nose. Curly hair encircled his head like a fuzzy halo. His bare arms were thick and well-muscled.

"Godspeed," said Bear with not the slightest hint of urgency. "Peradventure, would you be sailing soon?"

"Aye. When we load."

"Where might you be sailing to?"

"Flanders."

"Bringing wool?" said Bear, with a nod to the barrels.

"We are," said the man. "Is there some matter here for you in all this? I've no time to gossip. We must sail at dawn."

Bear advanced a few more steps. "My name is Bear, and I, along with my children"—he gestured back toward us—

"are—may God grace our way—seeking passage to Flanders."

"Are you now? For what reason?"

"I'm a weaver," said Bear. "I'm seeking employment there."

"And I'm short two men, and eager to load, but the attackers destroyed the machinery. You look strong enough. If you lend a hand I can offer a voyage for a shilling. With luck we should take no more than a day or two. But I'll want to sail with the morning's tide. A good wind is promised. If we catch it, we'll make fair speed."

"We're more than willing," said Bear.

Bear offered the coins that Benedicta had given us, and then the three of us took to rolling the barrels into the cog, which, I hoped, would take us to safety.

I was very tense as we worked, fearing those who sought Bear would appear at any moment. If Bear felt the same, he did not show it, but turned to the task at hand. I don't know what aid Troth or I provided, but we pushed and rolled by his side, one heavy barrel at a time.

Once all the tuns had been lowered into the hold, a lid was placed over the hatchway and hammered in with bits of rope stuffed in the cracks. "To keep the seawater out," Bear explained.

"Will none get in?" asked Troth.

"It will surely be all around us. But, God willing, not over us."

When the barrels had been loaded, we all, at the ship-master's request, put our shoulders to the cog's bow, and shoved her free from the sand into the water. With the ship afloat, Bear waded into the water and hoisted Troth and I onto the deck. Then he clambered aboard.

We were now on the cog. A line ran to the shore from the boat's stern and was tied round a stone. Then one of the mariners went forward and heaved out the iron anchor from the bow. Between the two lines the cog held steady in mid-river. The sail was furled. In this fashion we were ready to depart at first light, winds—and God—willing.

With the boat secure, I watched the master's three com-panions go off, moving up the shingle, past the remnants of the beach fire and into town through the Landgate. That left the ship's master and us on board. Night was now with us.

The master called out to Bear, "Come, my good man, present yourself and your brood so I can see what manner of folk you might be."

We approached the man where he stood at the stern. He held up a lit lantern and gazed at us.

"Your daughter is afflicted," he said.

"Only to those who would see it so," returned Bear.

"Does she bring bad luck?"

"As Jesus is my witness," said Bear, his hand resting on her shoulder, "only good."

"Well then, as God wills it," murmured the man, putting his lantern to one side. "Now then, I thank you for your assistance and your coin. I suppose you'll want to stay and sleep here till the dawn."

"If it pleases," said Bear.

"Best do," said the master. "We'll want to bestir ourselves as early as possible. If you can find a place to sleep by the bow, midst the chaff, be free to do so. I fear I've no food for you. I'll be here," he said, meaning the ship's castle.

"We thank you for your kindness," said Bear.

We took ourselves to the bow. There, upon the rough planking, was all manner of things strewn about: coils of old, rough rope; rusty hammers; axes; rotting rags; plus other things I did not know. We cleared some space next to the capstan, the better to spend the night. The master, having wrapped himself in a blanket, had doused his lamp so the only light came from smoldering coals on the shore. Above were naught but stars and a crescent moon.

"Will those men," I whispered to Bear, "the ones who came for you, not search here too?"

"Let's pray not," said Bear.

"But those other men," I said, "from the boat, they went into town. I saw them pass through the Landgate."

"What of it?"

"Might they not go to a tavern?" I pressed. "Might not those brotherhood men go to such places and ask for you? And did you not once say to me that you were like a cardinal in a flock of ravens?"

In the darkness I heard Bear laugh. "Ah, Crispin—Saint Benedicta of Milan—she who looks after students—surely has blessed you. I daresay you are right and I'm wrong."

"Then shouldn't we keep watch?"

"We should. As an act of penance for my mindless ways I'll stand the first part. I'll wake you in good time, and you, in turn, can wake Troth."

"Who will I look for?" asked Troth.

"Three men, I suppose," I said.

Having agreed, Bear hauled himself up. As he did, he put his hand to his head. "My hat!" he cried.

"Where is it?"

"I left it at the inn." He looked the picture of misery. "I've half a mind to fetch it."

"You mustn't," I said.

"God's truth," he agreed. "But it gives me reason—

someday—to return." That said, he went to lean upon the deck walls midship so he could observe the shore. I watched as he stood there, slumped, thinking, I supposed, of his precious hat. Then Troth and I lay down and gave ourselves over to sleep in rhythm to the gently bobbing cog.

Troth dozed off first. I lay awake, staring into the sky and the multitude of stars. "All will be well," I kept saying to myself. "It will."

24

EXACTLY WHEN IT WAS that Bear woke me I don't know. With the bells having been stolen from Rye's church, it was hard to know the time. Regardless, he woke me with a shake, saying, "By your leave, lad, it's your watch now."

Though sleepy, I forced myself up. "Did you see anything?" I asked.

"Only the stars and moon," he returned. But as he lay down, he placed Benedicta's dagger by his side.

I stumbled to my feet and went to the place where I'd seen Bear keep his watch. Once there, I leaned upon the deck walls and looked toward the beach. The fire had gone out. Not so much as an ember glowed. Such light as there was came from above—just enough to vaguely see by.

I had not been there long when Troth joined me. "It's not your time," I said.

"I could not sleep," she replied.

We stood quietly, side by side, looking at the darkness.

"Where is Flanders?" asked Troth.

"I don't know," I said, even though I recalled Bear saying the Flemish were a mercantile people and that he did not trust them.

"Will we be able to come back?"

"Of course."

"How?"

"The way we go."

"Will we be safe there?"

"Safer than here."

After a long while during which neither of us did more than breathe, she said, "Aude told me you were good."

"How would she know?"

"Aude knew everything. Crispin . . . I'm sad."

"Why?"

"I'm leaving her."

"Perhaps . . . perhaps she is in a better place."

"Where?"

I thought for a moment, then said, "That place you spoke of, beyond the edge of the world."

For a while Troth said nothing, though in the darkness I could hear her breathing hard. It was as if there was some struggle in her. From the folds of her clothing she pulled out the sprig of hawthorn tree she had taken. She held it over the water as if to drop it.

"You should keep it," I said.

"Why?"

"It binds you to your love."

She gazed at it, and then put it back in her safe place.

We spoke no more. Teased by the river swells, the cog heaved gently. Standing there, staring into the night, I dozed. I woke with a start when I heard Troth say, "Crispin, three men have come!"

"Where?" I whispered.

"There," she said, pointing toward the dim shore.

Gradually I perceived what she had seen. Three men were walking along the beach. One of them held a small torch, hardly more than a fist of fire. But it was enough light for me to recognize the man we had met beyond Great Wexly: the archer who had wounded Bear.

On the instant, I ducked. Troth did the same. "Is that

them?" she asked me quietly.

"Yes. Stay low," I said and eased myself up, just enough to spy.

By God's good grace, the three men paused at the first cog they came to, the one farther upstream. The torch-bearer held up the light, while the archer hauled himself onto the boat. Then he reached down, and took hold of the torch. The other men boarded.

I could see them move about, searching. I was sure when they found that cog deserted, they would come to us.

Trying to think what to do, I recalled Bear's dagger.

"Troth," I hissed. "Keep watching that boat." I hurried to where Bear slept. Seeing his dagger by the faint gleam of its iron blade, I took it up and went back to Troth.

"Are they still on that cog?" I said.

"Yes."

"Call if they start to come."

"Where are you going?"

"Not far." I crept to our boat's stern. I could just see the ship's master curled up on a blanket against one side, his curly hair exposed. I searched about, seeking where the rope—the one connected to the shoreline—was attached. It was not hard to find.

Working silently, I used the dagger to saw upon the

multistranded rope. I made certain not to work at one spot, wanting the cut to be as jagged as possible—like a rip.

The boat's movement helped; it kept the rope taut, with an occasional sharp tug that made my cutting easier. Sure enough, the rope began to fray. Fingers of cord sprang up. When the boat gave a sudden lurch, the rope split. Instantly pulled by the tide, the cog swung out. Drawing upon its bow anchor, it floated out into the middle of the river.

It was all so gentle the ship's master did not stir.

I went back to where Troth was and looked back.

"How did you do that?" she asked.

I grinned and held up the dagger. "Where are those men?" I asked.

"Still on that other boat," she said.

Not for long. As we watched, they quit the first cog and climbed down onto the beach.

I gripped the dagger.

We watched as they advanced along the shore. If they had expected to find our cog where it had been, they were surprised.

Holding up their torch, they stood upon water's edge. I could hear the faint murmur of their voices. Unable to reach our cog, they soon departed, trudging toward town through the Landgate.

"Jesus is kind," I said. Even so, Troth and I remained on watch for the remainder of the night.

25

HE FIRST STREAK of dawn had just appeared with a cock's crow when the ship's three mariners returned. They had to swim to the cog, which they did with many a curse. The Master, much perplexed, assumed the rope had frayed by itself. No accusations were made.

Troth and I gave a hurried, whispered explanation to Bear. "Saint Bathildis," he said with a grin, "who protects children, must follow your footsteps very near."

I was full of satisfaction.

Meanwhile, the mariners were busy, one climbing the mast until he perched cross-legged atop the sail yardarm.

"Let it fall!" cried the master. The knots of cord that held the sail were undone. The great square sheet of Brittany canvas unrolled, revealing alternating stripes of red and white. Two mariners caught the ropes at each corner, and tied them to the deck. The master threw his weight upon the rudder stick. The cog swung about. The sail crackled and filled with the morning's breeze.

Now Bear, along with Troth and I, were called to turn the capstan so that the anchor—a two-pronged hook of iron—was hauled up. As the anchor lifted from the water, the cog began to glide down the river, into the lower bay, then quickly into the sea itself. We had left Rye behind.

Looking back, I swear I saw three men upon the shore looking out as we went on.

"We're safe," I said to Troth, full of pride.

With the ship's master holding the rudder rod in strong and easy hands, we sailed out upon the rolling swell of sea. The cog's blunt prow smacked the waves with a steady, splashing rhythm. The great, square sail snapped. The air was suffused with a salt-heavy dampness. Several squawking birds followed in our wake only to fall behind, indifferent to our fate. The green of England dropped away rapidly, grow-ing ever smaller to my eyes.

How passing strange it was that though I was doing nothing, I was being carried somewhere at enormous speed. It was hard for me to know if the land was shifting or if it was we that moved. It was as if the earth had become unhinged and detached, moving several different ways at once.

In truth, all too soon, our cog crested the waves with such pitch and yaw that I felt as though I was always falling. The sound of the waves came with a repetitious roaring monotony as if the voice of eternity were trumpeting into my ears. My need to cling to something *not* moving was great, but nothing on that ship remained still.

Increasingly queasy, I stood near the ship's master, clinging to the rail with both hands while taking great gulps of pungent air. Twice I purged my stomach, and in so doing, any further desire to be a mariner.

I looked round for Bear. He was forward on the deck, alone. He, like Troth, had his eyes turned toward the receding shore. His face bore such melancholy as I had never seen on him before. Had I wrongly urged our departure? Was it a mistake to have left England? But when I recalled those brotherhood men and Bear's weakness, I knew we had to go. It *was* right, I told myself, then turned about and cast my eyes upon the sea.

What I saw was a numbing expanse of gray sea and sky, a world of utter emptiness, spotted by frothy white. I was upon a world I never knew, going to a place I could not imagine, in a fashion I could but dream. I was excited, frightened, and bewildered, alarmed to be leaving what was old, proud to be doing something new, eager to see what was yet to come, yet fearful that all the newness would find me wanting. And—recalling Troth's thoughts about the edge of the world—I felt much unease.

"Will we lose sight of land?" I called to the ship's master.

He looked round at me and pointed to the mast. "Climb that!" he shouted over the wind. "You'll never lose sight of land. On a clear day you can see for fifteen leagues."

I declined with a vigorous shake of my head.

Laughing, he shouted, "I take it you've never been to sea before!"

I shook my head anew, afraid to open my mouth for fear of what might come out.

"God's eyes!" he exclaimed, grinning wide. "You need not worry. We'll never be far from some shore. Then again, you mustn't get too close to land."

"Why?"

"A sudden change of wind and tide—and this narrow sea is infamous for such—and you'll get sucked in and wrecked. A watery grave is a sodden place for a Christian soul to rest. Can you swim?" he asked, his eyes so merry they crinkled.

Refusing to be teased I said, "Do you often make this voyage?"

"There's always wool to be brought and cloth to return."

"Are we close to Flanders?"

"We'll sail up the Kentish coast. Reaching the Dover light we'll cross to Normandy in France—that's the narrowest passage—then northward along that coast until we come to Flanders."

Remembering how France was the one place Bear did *not* want to go, I said, "Will we touch France?"

"Not if God is kind."

"Do you still think our voyage will take two days?"

He grinned. "Once it took twelve."

"Twelve!" I cried—and we without food.

He licked two dirty fingers and held them in the air. "The wind, my lad," he said. "God's great breath has us at His mercy. Confess your sins!" he said with glee. "Some never reach land at all."

I swallowed hard. "Will it get rougher than it is now?"

He snorted. "This is *smooth*. So best get to your knees and pray. Blessed Saint Nicholas is kind to sailors and infants. And if he fails you, there's always Saint Jude for lost causes."

As we sailed on I had an urgent need to sit. To stand. To keep holding on. To let go. To hide. To do all those things at once yet dare not allow myself any excess movement. With my back pressed hard against the castle wall, my head bowed against my knees, I kept my eyes shut. Blackness somehow helped. Even so, the continual rise and fall of the cog was a constant reminder as to where I was and what was happening.

When Troth joined me I noted she was not ill. "You're a better mariner than I," I said.

"My herbs would cure you," she said.

"Are you sorry we came?" I asked.

She shook her head, but would say no more.

From time to time my sickness eased, but the slightest extra movement tumbled my guts. Having nothing better to do, I was content to watch the mariners at their tasks.

Now and again, one of them flung out chips of wood from the bow and observed them traverse the whole ship's length. Using his fingers, the man counted the time it took for the bits to flow past the boat, after which he would call the numbers to the master. Other times he would heave a lump of lead—connected to a line—overboard, then haul it up and cry how far it had plunged before hitting bottom. Sometimes he even touched his tongue to the lead. When I asked why he did these things, he explained that the flow of the chips allowed him to know how fast they sailed. That dropping the lead revealed the water's depth. As for the tasting, he had sailed the course so often his mariner's tongue informed him over which deep-water sand they sailed. In combination, these things could tell him just where they were. I could only marvel at his cunning.

After more time passed, I forced myself to stand and look about. To my dismay I could see no more land—nothing but the heavy, empty sea.

"Where are we?" I asked in sudden dread.

The master, who found much amusement in my woeful state, looked up into the sky at the pale sun, and finally said, "Still afloat."

I sat back down in haste. Would our voyage—I wondered with no small misery—consist of two days or twelve?

Though there was nothing I could see—or know—to the contrary, I presumed we sailed easterly along the English coast toward Dover. As we beat on, however, stiffer winds bore down with increasing force. The master steered the cog first this way, now that, till my head was as uncorked as my stomach. The ship, which had appeared so substantial when beached at Rye, now seemed little more than an insignificant twig, tossed carelessly by wayward winds and water.

Bear, having roused himself from his private gloom,

worked with the mariners, heeding the increasingly insistent calls of the ship's master to tend the great sail, or to help keep the rudder steady when the sea began to swell.

Troth kept mostly to herself, standing by the rail, continuing to gaze upon the encircling sea. Whether she was looking back toward England, or searching for the sea's edge, I did not know. I was much too concerned with my tumbled guts to pay heed to anyone but myself. Thus does a large private misery make public compassion small.

Whether we made any progress I could not tell, not even if we reached Dover's Head. My vague sensation was that we were being beaten back. With increasing frequency, the cog pitched and rocked. Waves began to break across the deck, soaking all, leaving us shuddering with the sopping cold, while sluicing away anything not tied down. The mariners struggled to keep knots taut.

In the lowering gloom, they hung three lit lamps: upon the mast, on the bow, on the stern. Even as they did, the winds grew stiffer. The sea rose. The waves lashed. The sky began to darken balefully. It took three men to hold the rudder. The master filled his commands with angry shouts and oaths, upbraiding the Devil while urging his men to tasks with a growing fury that filled me with rising apprehension.

I began to say my prayers in earnest.

Bear called to Troth, and the two of them sat by me, he in the middle.

The mariners huddled by the master, darting forward now and again to obey shouted commands.

"Does night always bring such storms at sea?" I asked.

"God's breath, Crispin," Bear exclaimed. "It's not night yet. But when you travel by sea, storms are part of the journey. Know that God is in his heaven, and the master is at his helm. We can do no better than that. These storms don't last long."

Though he spoke with confidence, I knew I was frightened, not that I would admit to it.

Bear, as if knowing my mind, said, "No harm will come if we stay together."

He extended his arms round Troth and me, and drew us closer. Somewhat comforted, I asked, "Bear, are you sorry we've come?"

"We had no choice," he said.

"We'll go back," I said, much as I had to Troth.

"In truth," said Bear, "a wise man has as many hopes as reasons."

"We *will*," I insisted.

"God grant it," he said, grim again.

26

S THE SHIP continued to toss and roll, Bear left us to crawl about on all fours. Reaching the bow, he found a length of wet rope, dragged it back, and wrapped it round us and then to a rail. We were held fast.

"Why did you do that?" Troth asked.

"So we won't be washed away," Bear told her.

I looked at Troth. Her eyes were on some inner vision I could not fathom.

When I turned to the master, I saw that he too had lashed himself to the rudder pole.

As the turbulence grew greater, it became darker still. Such light as we had came from the three small lanterns and was hardly more than a blur, like memories of distant days.

The winds howled. The waves crashed. My soul felt naked. Then a damp mist fell heavily about us like wet wool only to transform itself to drizzle. I opened my mouth and sucked in the sweet water to cleanse my foul tongue. But all too soon the rain turned heavy, pelting the deck like some mad drummer's call to arms. It seemed to compete with the ocean—as if to make of the air another sea. We could do naught but compress ourselves, trying, by being smaller, to hide from the storm's assault.

Bursts of lightning tore through the dark with jagged clawlike streaks, followed by a thunderous rolling that made the skies tremble. The same flashing exposed the mariners' faces, making them look like pallid skulls.

In this hurly-burly void, the cog leaped and fell with ever-increasing frenzy, twisting and climbing, only to drop into what felt to be a void. Sometimes we canted so far over I thought we must capsize. Even when the ship righted herself, the sea flowed across the deck with abandon. The lantern lights spit and hissed. The wind cried mournfully, rising and falling like tormented souls bewailing their fate at being left to wallow in an endless sea.

At some point, I hardly knew when, the three lanterns were swallowed whole and with them went the last sparks of light—and so it seemed, any hope of life itself.

My heart hammered. My breath grew short. Our hair streamed. Our clothing clung to us like sopping winding sheets. Sure we were about to perish, I prayed incessantly, confessing to everything while vowing I would perform multitudes of holy penance—if only God would show His clemency. A crying Troth pressed herself against Bear's chest. I clutched him too. Oh, vanity to think tears could be measured in such a storm!

As the storm rioted on, Bear held us tight. At one point he began to sing a raucous, vulgar soldier's song that dared do battle with the weather.

Each moment I was sure the storm had reached its final fury. Each time it surpassed what came before. Once, in a blast of lightning, I saw the four mariners struggling with the rudder, their fear palpable. Bear squeezed us that much more tightly and roared on with his ferocious song.

"I want Aude!" I heard Troth cry aloud.

"I'm here, Troth!" cried Bear. "I'm here!"

Though I tried to keep my eyes closed, crackling lightning flashes caused me to blink them open. As the black night was torn asunder, I saw that our sail had split into several parts, and was now flapping like so many flags—each one an offer of surrender.

Then, midst the howling wind and drenching rains, came the cry: "Man over!"

I don't know if any attempts to save the mariner were made. It seemed unlikely. But shortly after, as if a human sacrifice had been wanted and delivered bodily to the raging gods of storm, the weather began to subside. Though the winds roared on, the rain eased. The cog pitched less.

"Is the storm gone?" Troth cried.

"I pray so," said Bear.

As if to provide a last salute, a final burst of booming lightning struck, and in that blast of brightness, I could see that there was no one at the rudder.

We were alone.

In utter darkness, as the rain continued to fall and the wind to blow, I sensed the cog was still moving apace, but where driven I could hardly know. The boat, the water, the wind, my despair, all was one. The only sounds I heard were the continual *slip-slap* of waves as the cog skipped along.

Adding to my sense of doom was the fact that Bear did nothing but hold us mutely. No more songs. No more words. But by Saint Jude, what could he or any of us do? We were alone in God's great hands—if He only would hold us. My private sickness faded only to be replaced by the greater dread of being lost—lost by life, lost by the world, lost by God.

Gradually, the rain dissolved into mist. A sullen dawn suffused the air, so dismal, so weak, I could just barely see my own hands. The world had turned phantom.

More light came. The mist thinned. I could see my feet, the deck, and then much of the cog. I saw one of the mariners lay stretched midship, his foot tangled in a rope. His lifeless hand flopped with the boat's random movement.

The mast with its shredded sail was still erect, although the topmost parts melted into mist. Where the rudder rod had been was . . . nothing—just a jagged splinter of wood.

Bear's rope had saved us. What, I wondered, had it saved us for?

He slept, snoring slightly. His beard was dripping wet. His face looked wan, and despite so much sea and rain, so parched I could see his cheekbones. It brought on a sudden memory of how I'd first found him—a mountain of flesh, a great barrel of a fellow, whose arms and legs were as thick as tree limbs, and with a great stomach before all. How much of that—waxlike—had melted.

Troth pressed against Bear's chest, soaked. Her eyes were open.

"Are you all right?" I whispered.

She nodded, shivering, and squeezed herself closer to Bear.

"Bear!" I called.

"Alive," he muttered.

With the cog now at greater ease and rocking gently, I loosened the knotted rope. Once free, I reached up, took hold of the rail, and stood on unsteady feet.

A deep, damp gray fog enclosed us. I could barely see the water flowing by.

I kept watching for something to tell me where we were. Were we near England? Flanders? I had no idea. But I had been drained of all desire to become a mariner. If I never set foot on another ship, it would be soon enough for me.

As our speed decreased, the light increased. The mist swirled. In places it parted. What I saw caused me to stare with disbelief. Looming through the mist and fog—as if rising from the sea itself—were towering cliffs of rosy stone.

As God is holy, it was as if we had truly reached the rock-hard boundaries of the mortal world—the true edge of the world.

27

 EAR!" I cried. "Look!"

Not fully awake, he shifted with a slight groan.

"Bear, you must look!"

He breathed deeply and blinked up at me with bleary, red-rimmed eyes. His clothing, like mine, was wet and dripping.

After running a finger round his mouth as if to rid it of a fetid taste, he rubbed his pale face, and raked a hand through his tangled, wet beard. Only when he leaned forward did he recall that he was still bound by the soggy rope he'd tied. With sea-puckered fingers he teased the knot apart. He stood slowly, stiffly.

Troth—equally wet—slipped out of the rope. Bear extended a hand so that she might stand. Only then did the two of them look out. If I understood their faces, they were as startled as I had been.

Stone cliffs seemed to be moving in and out of the mist on mighty hinges. Mist hovered so low it was impossible to know just how high these cliffs were. That they were jagged, hard-edged and rosy in cast, I could see. By contrast, the water surrounding us was mostly calm, dark blue flecked with white foam, clotted with green weeds. Here and there, black rocks stuck up. From aloft I could hear birds— or what I thought were birds—squawking. I half expected dragons with yawning maws to rise up and swallow us whole.

"Where are we?" I asked with awe.

"I have no idea," said Bear as he stared about, his voice just as full of wonder.

"Could we be back in England?" I said.

"We could."

"Or is this Flanders?" asked Troth.

"Anywhere," said Bear, shaking his head.

"Perhaps," I offered, "it's the end of the sea."

Bear shrugged, and turned to survey the cog. I followed his gaze. We were still moving, but very slowly. Oddly enough, the cog was in perfect order. All that had been loose had been washed away. Bear's dagger—gone. Our sack with the recorder—gone. Our fire-making tools—gone. There was just the mariner lying there. Bear went to him, and put a hand on his chest.

"Is he alive?" I called.

Bear's response was to make the sign of the cross and back away.

"Where are the others?" Troth asked.

Bear shrugged. "Lost. Swept over." He began to wander about the boat looking for what I knew not.

Troth and I remained side by side at the rail, gazing up at the cliffs. The cog, eased on by a rising tide, was drawing closer to the cliffs. Three times we struck rocks. Each time the cog recoiled, only to edge further in, the ship's hull making a scraping noise. Finally, there came a harsh, grinding sound as the cog's keel struck bottom, sounding like the rattling breath of a dying man.

The ship shuddered. It seemed to settle. We stopped moving. All that remained of the torturous journey was a gentle rocking which matched the wash of waves. These waves flicked against the ship like kitten tongues as though to soothe the remnants of our terror.

"There's the top!" I cried as the mist lifted further. The cliffs reached some two hundred feet over our heads.

It was possible now to see that the cog was in a little inlet, a finger of the sea, surrounded on three sides by rock. At the lower levels of the cliff I could see boulders piled high. The boat—with us upon it—had been nudged there by the movement of the ocean, wedged between the high stone walls with no room for turning about.

Bear went to the bow of the boat. "Even the anchor is gone," he announced.

"Will the boat stay?" I wondered.

"We've been brought in by a rising tide," said Bear. "I suppose the tides could pluck her out again."

"Will the other mariners be found?" asked Troth. She was looking down at the dead one.

"Not in this world," said Bear. "Are you as exhausted as I?" he asked.

We both nodded.

"Thirsty and hungry, too, I suppose." Bear went to the

hatch, and labored to pry it open. We worked with him, pulling out the caulking. Once we managed to get it open, Bear stuck his head down.

"Dry as stone," he announced. "That caulking saved us. If the hold had flooded . . . But unless we eat wool there's no food."

"Was there a rudder?" I asked.

"I don't see one. I think I saw another sail."

"What will we do?" I asked, my voice hushed.

Bear looked out on the shore. "We'd best get off while we can. My feet would like to find some solid soil. Then we'll need to climb those cliffs to learn where God has brought us."

"What about him?" I said, indicating the dead mariner.

"The living first," said Bear.

He clambered over the cog's side, and dropped heavily into the water with a splash. As it reached his waist, I could see him shiver with the chill. Turning, he let Troth jump down into his outstretched arms, set her on his shoulders, and waded toward the shore.

I leaped after them, feet first. The cold water clutched my chest and squeezed my breath away.

Walking as best I could, I followed after Bear, arms over my head. It was rocky beneath the water, forcing me to go with care, seeking my balance as best I could. Once I slipped, and for my pains was soaked to my hair and draped in weeds.

Closer in, Bear set Troth atop a huge boulder upon which he pulled himself. The two began to make for real land, crawling and walking toward the shore, jumping from stone to stone. I came after, pausing now and again to look up at the cliffs, wondering how we would climb them.

We reached the shore. The beach was a narrow, rocky place, embedded with great boulders—no doubt fallen from above. Bowls of fine sand lay between. Seaweed was abundant. White oyster shells were scattered everywhere. With each passing moment, the air cleared further, revealing blue sky and a warm, bright sun. Birds called like rasping angels. Though it seemed odd to find the land so firm, I was grateful to be there.

How extraordinary, I thought, to be *some* place without knowledge of where one was. I considered anew the possibility that we *had* died. Perhaps Heaven was no more than this unknown shore. Then I had to remind myself, it was equally possible we had come to Hell.

Bear was gazing at the walls of stone that confronted us. Troth and I watched him.

"That may be a way up, there," he finally said, pointing

to what looked to be a crevice in the cliff. He went toward it. Troth and I clambered after. As he walked, he stumbled slightly, enough to strike his knee against a stone. He swore, rubbed it, but labored on, limping again.

When we reached the spot that Bear had seen, it proved to be a cleft that went some ways upward. It was hard to see how far it reached.

Bear stood before it, so hesitant I could read his exhaustion from the way he fixed his shoulders. In protecting us during the night, he had become much spent.

Knowing he would not admit to it, but that we had to go forward, I simply pushed past him. "I'll go," I announced. And without waiting for Bear's permission, I began to climb.

28

Y ASCENT went easily at first, hardly more than walking up a steep incline. Gradually, however, the passageway began to narrow, and became increasingly steep. I soon found myself pressed close on either side by hard and jagged rock. Sharp edges were enough to score my hands, though they did provide places for my fingers to grasp.

Fearful of falling, I glanced down only to be frightened by the height I'd reached. Bear and Troth, standing below, seemed distant. The cog was equally remote. No other land was in sight save some rocks that broke the water's surface.

"Are you all right?" Bear shouted.

"Yes!" I called, though I hardly felt it.

Having no choice—other than to drop—I kept on, moving grip by grip, pushing as much as pulling. Every part of my body trembled with the struggle, aware as I was of the likelihood of falling and dashing my head on the rocks below.

But with God's blessing I came to a place where the climb was not so steep. I was able to crawl upward on hands and knees, not caring that they were battered. My sense of relief gave me a surge of strength. With quicker progress, I reached the top. Once there, I looked out upon the land we'd reached. To my surprise, there was no surprise.

It was much like land I had seen before: naught but rolling green fields and at the distance of perhaps half a league, a line of trees. As for any hint or clue as to *where* we were, I saw not one jot. Passing strange, to have come so far across the world only to see what was familiar.

After my quick look, I returned the way I came, or at least the last, easy part. Leaning over the cliff, I cried, "I reached the top!"

"What's there?"

"Nothing!"

"*Nothing?*" exclaimed Bear.

"Fields. Grass!"

After a moment, Bear said, "We'll come along."

"Take care!" I warned.

Troth came first. She scampered as agile as any goat. If she had any fears or difficulty, I saw them not. In fact, it seemed she reached the top in half the time it took me.

With Bear it was quite otherwise. I could hear him swearing and grunting his painstaking way. As Troth and I looked down there were moments—more than a few—that we held our breath, fearful he would fall.

At length, Bear reached the top, puffing mightily, sweating hard. I led them along for the remainder of the way so they could see what I saw.

Troth and Bear gazed out over the open fields. I looked with them. No one spoke, until I asked Bear, "Do you know where we are now?"

"No," he replied. "Not at all." He sat down, breathing heavily. "By Saint Luke, I'm weary."

"I don't like it here," Troth announced. She had been gazing about.

"Why?" I demanded.

"It makes me uneasy."

"There are plenty of places in England where you won't see people," Bear said. "What troubles you?"

She only shook her head.

"Those trees over there," I said. "I could explore them."

Bear did not respond. The look on his face was of great fatigue. He was favoring his wounded arm again. "Go if you choose," he said. "But be cautious. I need to try and rest a bit."

"I'll go with Crispin," said Troth.

"Keep safe," muttered Bear, who had laid himself out on his back, face to sun, arms spread wide.

Troth and I waited. It took only moments before Bear fell asleep. Without another word, Troth and I turned and started across the fields.

I found pleasure in striding over ground that did not move, pushing through grass almost as tall as Troth. The grass was wonderfully sweet to smell and, here and there, yellow flowers rose as if to remind us we had returned to a more loving earth. With the sun's golden glow beating on our faces, it almost seemed a paradise. When I thought of where we had been, no contrast could have been greater. Rejoicing, I breathed deeply, and allowed myself to give thanks to God for His mercy.

As we went further, I glanced back in the direction from

where we'd come. To my surprise the ocean seemed to have vanished—as if it didn't exist. I had to remind myself that it was merely below the cliff. I didn't see Bear either.

A touch from Troth brought me out of my prayerful musings.

"Crispin," she said, looking up at me with her solemn eyes.

"What?"

"On the ship—during the storm—I thought we were going to die."

I stopped walking. "I thought so, too," I said.

"It was Bear," she said, "who saved us."

"I know."

She looked back where he was. "But," she whispered, "it exhausted him."

"If we care for him," I said, "he'll regain his strength."

She hesitated before saying, "I'm not so sure."

"I promise you he will!" The words came out angrily.

She turned and went on silently. I ran after her and we went on toward the trees, neither of us speaking. It was as if we had quarreled.

As I drew closer to the trees, I could see that they were not very tall, and were twisted into bizarre shapes. It was as if winds and storms coming off the sea had shaped them.

We were perhaps twenty yards from them when I suddenly halted. "Look there!" I cried, pointing up. "Birds."

Black birds were flying over the trees in a circular movement.

"What about them?" asked Troth.

"They're fleeing something. Bear taught me to look for that."

"It could be an animal."

"Or a person." I looked back. With Bear sleeping on the ground, there was no sign of him. Knowing how tired he was, I had no wish to disturb him—less so if there was nothing to relate. "We'd best first find what it is," I said.

Cautious about going directly to where the birds flew, I led the way to one side. In moments, we were among the trees, where it was easy to be concealed. Once there I changed our direction, going where I thought the birds had flown. We moved from tree to tree quietly. Then—unmistakably—we heard the whinny of a horse.

We halted. From Troth's look, I knew she had heard it, too.

"Where did it come from?" I whispered.

"There," she said, and crept forward silently, somewhat crouched, head turned slightly to catch any sounds—the image of Aude. Suddenly she stood, extended one arm, and whispered, "There!"

I looked. There were three horses.

They were powerful beasts, destriers, the kind of horses used by soldiers. Tethered, they were at their ease, eating grass. All had leather harnesses without any decorations, reins over necks, bits in their mouths. There were three saddles stacked on a stump, one atop the other. The saddles had high seats that allowed a rider to ride standing. There were protective pommels too.

Troth looked to me as if I could provide some explanation.

"Soldiers' horses," I whispered.

I sniffed, sensing a faint smell of roasting meat.

We stood in place, searching for the people we knew must be near. Farther in among the trees I noticed a two-wheeled cart, and not far from it, an ox.

Suddenly, Troth began to move.

"Troth!" I called. "Don't!"

Ignoring me, she went on. I thought to hold her back, but then I recalled the time when I first saw her in the woods: she had been as silent as any spirit—all but invisible. Still, I watched her go with sudden trepidation. How hard, I thought, if something happened to her!

Then—as if one thought followed from the other—I thought of what she had said of Bear: that he had never fully recovered from his time in Great Wexly or the arrow wound. Then we had had to flee. The storm had worn him more. He was much weaker. It would not have surprised me if he still had a fever.

Standing there, in a world I did not know, Troth before me, Bear behind—both out of sight—I had the keenest sense of how much these two—so different one from each other—made up my world. From that flowed an almost overwhelming sense that loving meant I must also know what it must be to lose them.

I don't know how long I waited nervously, but Troth returned as suddenly and as silently as she had gone.

"Did you find anything?" I asked.

"Over there," she said, pointing. "People." Not knowing how to count, she held her hand up many times.

"Forty? Men? Women?"

"Men."

"What are they?"

"Some had swords. Some wore helmets. I saw bows leaning against a tree. There were poles with metal points."

"Did you hear them speak?"

"I wasn't close enough. Do you want me to go back?"

"Show them to me."

She set off and I followed. Within moments, we covered some forty or fifty yards, keeping ourselves hidden among the trees. Troth knelt and pointed.

Sure enough, perhaps forty men were gathered in a clearing. For the most part, the men were young, though I saw one with graying hair. They were dirty, tattered, and ill-shaven. Exposed arms had scars. Among them I saw no smiles, not one gentle face. No two were dressed the same. A few wore helmets, some of the kettle-hat kind, others, open-faced basinets. These helmets were dented and rusty. One or two had jagged holes. All the men wore shoes or boots, but no two jackets were alike. There was some metal plating worn, much tarnished. Some soldiers carried bullock daggers on their hips, some carried swords. A few shields, dented and without design or insignia, had been propped against a tree. I saw a pole with a banneret leaning against a tree, but could not make out its heraldry.

Some of the men were resting, backs against trees. One man had his eyes shut, sleeping. Others lay stretched out on the ground, perhaps also asleep. Most were standing, sharpening swords, or working arrows. It was as if they were preparing for some action. One small man tended a fire upon which sat a large pot. It was that which we had smelled.

I spied yet another man sitting against a tree. The soldiers seemed to defer to him. I took him to be their captain. He did not look to be very different from the others, though beneath his quilted jacket I spied what appeared to be chain mail covering his chest and arms.

"What are they doing?" whispered Troth.

"I don't know. Resting. Preparing."

"For what?"

"Battle."

Then the one I took to be their captain lifted an arm, and called, "Jason! Come here."

They were Englishmen.

29

OR A MOMENT, I was tempted to rush forward and announce ourselves. I even took a step in that direction, but Troth held me back.

"You don't know who they are," she said. "We need to get Bear."

Deciding she was right, we hurried back over the field, running once we were clear of the trees. Bear was as we'd left him, asleep.

We sat by his side, waiting for him to waken. From time to time, I stood and looked toward the trees. Though no one came, I was increasingly anxious.

"I think we should get him up," I finally said and shook his foot.

Bear stirred. "Good morrow," he muttered.

I leaned over his face. "Bear," I said. "We've found people."

"Where?" he said, without opening his eyes.

"Back among those trees."

"What are they?"

"They speak English."

"Are we in England, then?" he said, sounding relieved.

"I don't know. Bear, they're soldiers."

"God's grief," he sighed, opening his eyes. "How many?"

"Say, forty."

"No more?"

I told him what we had seen.

He pushed himself up and rubbed his face, as if to restore his blood. Looking at him, I had a thought I never had before: he seemed old. I would have sworn his beard had streaks of gray.

"No more than forty?" he asked again.

"It seems."

"By Saint Barnabas . . . No more than that?" he asked a third time.

"Why is the number important?"

"A troop of just a few soldiers—unattached—could be a free company."

"Should we fear them?" asked Troth.

"In truth, if we were in England," said Bear, "they might be just going home."

I said, "Where else could we be?"

He marked the places on his fingers: "England. France. Normandy. Brittany. Aquitaine. Flanders. Navarre."

He remained sitting, sometimes glancing at the sun, or at the distant trees. He even studied one of his large hands. At last he heaved himself up. "Come along," he said.

"Where?"

"God's bones! Crispin, I've no stomach to meet with any soldiers. There is no safety with them."

"Bear," I blurted out, "there's no safety anywhere!"

"What's wrong with the soldiers?" said Troth. "Were you not one?"

He gave her a piercing glance, and seemed to swell with anger. She shrank back. The next moment, Bear's fury faded. "We'll get back on the cog," he said, "and try to ride her out. There was another sail in the hold. Perhaps I missed a rudder. If we are in England and we could get to some other place along this coast, I'd feel much better."

That said, he started back toward the cliff. Troth and I, following, exchanged worried looks. When we reached the cliff's edge, Bear knelt and looked out.

"In the name of the Father!" he roared. "I am being held captive by my sins!"

"Why?" I said. "What's the matter?"

"Look!" he said and pointed down.

Troth and I peered over the cliff. The cog, lifted by an incoming tide, had drifted out of the cove. She was bobbing out upon the sea.

He sat back heavily. "We could never reach her," he said in such a voice I thought he might cry.

With the cliff before us falling away so sharply, we dared do no more than sit and gaze out upon the ocean. There, the cog floated on the water's surface like an empty jug, moving still farther from the shore.

"By Saint Anthony," Bear muttered. "What kind of folly is it not to know if one is lost or saved?"

"Shall I go back to those soldiers?" I offered. "Learn more about them?"

"Crispin," Bear said, "if we are in England and they are English troops, we will have gained much. But if we are anywhere else, things might go badly."

"Why?" I asked.

"It's likely to be a free company. Thieves. Outlaws."

Troth said, "We could hide below."

"There is no hiding," said Bear, "from the will of God."

The wretchedness in his voice hurt my heart. It was much like that time in Rye when I told him of our pursuers: Bear in defeat. But then, I'd known of a way to escape.

Not now.

As we remained where we were, Troth and I exchanged anxious glances. I was sure she agreed we had to do something. Besides, it was a long while since we had eaten, and I was very hungry.

"The soldiers had food," I said.

"Crispin!" snapped Bear. "It's too dangerous."

"Bear," I cried, "we must do *something!*"

"Then pray to Saint Jude," said Bear.

"Who is that?" asked Troth.

"A saint who intervenes for lost causes," said Bear.

She turned to Bear. "Is our cause lost?"

He did not answer.

I looked across at Troth. She made another hand sign, which I understood to mean, "Wait."

Bear got up slowly, stiffly. "We'll all go," he said.

"Where?" I said.

"I don't think it matters. Let God decide."

Troth stood.

"Why don't you just rest here?" I said.

"By the breath of Jesus, Crispin!" Bear shouted. "Don't presume to decide for me or heave me on the refuse pile. Not yet."

"Bear—"

"Let's go!" he cried.

I pointed to the trees. "The soldiers are over there," I said, though I saw no sign of them.

"Eastward," said Bear. "Then we'll go north or south."

Troth looked at me.

"South," I said for no good reason.

We began to walk along the edge of the cliff. I went first, followed by Bear, then Troth. I went as fast as I could, but Bear was hobbling.

"Do you wish to me to go slower?" I asked.

"Crispin . . ." he growled.

We went on. But we had not gone for very long or far when Troth shouted, "Crispin!"

I turned and saw what she had seen. It was the troop of English soldiers. Led by three men on horseback, they had emerged from the trees in file. One of the horsemen held a banneret. Though faded, it bore a golden lion, rampant on a field of red.

We halted.

So did they. We had been discovered.

30

THE MAN on the lead horse, the one who seemed to be their captain, lifted an arm and pointed in our direction.

"God have mercy," Bear murmured, making the sign of the cross over his heart.

I made a movement toward the cliff only to have Bear clamp a hand to my arm to hold me fast. "Do you wish to be killed!" he hissed. "Stay!"

"But what are we to do?" I whispered.

"Be still," said Bear. "And say nothing."

The three horsemen drew swords and broke into a gal-
lop, driving their horses right at us. Having no doubt they
could dispatch us with ease if such was their will, I moved
closer to Bear, even as Troth drew nearer to me.

The lead man held his sword high, as if to strike. I
could not help but cower. Troth whimpered. But when the
horsemen came within five yards of us, they reined in hard.
Their trembling horses, nostrils flaring, arched their necks
and pawed the ground, as though wishing—and willing—
to trample us. The riders glowered.

I pressed closer to Bear.

"We are English!" Bear shouted. *"English!"* He held up
both hands, palms toward the soldiers, to show he held no
weapon.

The horsemen remained where they were, though the
lead rider, the one who held the sword, slowly lowered it. He
studied us, but it seemed to me that he was staring at Troth
in particular. "Who are you," he demanded, "and why are
you here?"

"We're shipwrecked pilgrims!" said Bear. "And by Saint
George, we have no notion where we are. Are we in
England?"

The question surprised the riders. They exchanged a few
words that we could not hear.

"You are in Brittany," the horseman called out. "France."

Bear grunted with displeasure.

The captain trotted forward, then stopped a few feet from where we stood, so near I could feel the hot breath of his horse. I noticed a dull iron helmet attached to his saddle.

The man looked down at us. He was short and stocky, yellow-haired, with broad shoulders. His face seemed squeezed from top to bottom, with deep-set eyes of hard gray, a thin mouth, large nose, and strong chin. I was reminded of an angry ox.

Beneath his gaze Troth drew her hair over her mouth and shrank back. Irritated by the man's presumption, I clenched my fists, though there was nothing I could do.

"What of this ship of yours?" he demanded.

"A cog," said Bear. "Out of Rye, for Flanders."

"What cargo?"

"Wool. We were overtaken by a storm that raged at sea last night. All perished, save us—thanks be to God."

"Where is it?"

"When the boat drifted close to shore, we managed to get off, but then it went out with the tide. You can still see it." Bear beckoned toward the sea.

The man gazed at Bear without responding—as if

measuring the words, or the man. He made no movement to see the boat. "What's your name?" he asked.

"Orson Hagar. I'm called Bear. Late of York. A traveling juggler and, if it pleases, pilgrim," he said for the second time. "These are my children."

The man turned his hard scrutiny on Troth again.

She looked down.

"The girl is unsightly," the man barked. "What afflicts her?"

"The rudeness of others," returned Bear with a touch of his old spirit.

Glowering, the captain leaned forward against his saddle pummel, staring at Bear, at me, Troth, then back to Bear, as if trying to make a decision. His two horse companions edged their mounts forward and waited on him.

He turned and said something to them, which I could not hear. Then he said to Bear, "The girl—she may be ugly, but is she nimble and strong?"

Bristling, Bear said, "She's my daughter. There's no need to insult her."

"By Saint Magnus!" cried the man. "Answer! Will she do as told?"

"If lawful."

The man sat back. "I make my own laws," he said.

Meanwhile, the rest of the soldiers had drawn in, forming a half circle about us so that there was no possible way of escape.

"Have you any money?" asked the captain.

"By Saint Alexius," said Bear, "having lost all, we are true beggars." He spoke with care, not wanting to give any offense. "May I ask who you are?"

"Richard Dudley. Of the Kentish Downs."

"You're a long way from home," said Bear.

"That's as may be."

"May I ask," said Bear, "if you serve King Richard?"

Dudley frowned. "Who is he?"

"By the grace of God, Master Dudley, he's England's king."

This caused a stir among the soldiers.

"What of King Edward?" Dudley demanded.

"God give him grace," said Bear. "He's been dead these two months. Richard of Bordeaux—his grandchild—has been crowned King."

Dudley made a hasty sign of the cross over his heart. "Our Edward was a great solider," he said.

"He was all of that," said Bear. "I served with his son, the Black Prince, at Poitiers. A famous victory."

"Did you?" cried Dudley. "Would that he were king."

He sat back in his saddle, appraising Bear in what seemed a new way. Bear's words made the soldiers nod and nudge each other and consider him with some respect. At least, they seemed to relax."

"Then you were a soldier," said Dudley.

"I was," said Bear. "But I grew old. And worn."

Dudley, sword hand lowered, leaned forward again, his free hand at rest. Once more he studied Troth, as if appraising her. He shifted back to Bear. "Well, then," he said with grin or grimace—hard to say which—"I offer you the good fortune of joining us."

"Your generosity does you honor," returned Bear. "Do I have a choice?"

"I think not," said Dudley.

"In the name of God, then," said Bear, "whom do you serve?"

That time, Dudley allowed himself a smile. "Myself," he said.

31

RICHARD DUDLEY called Bear to him, and told him to stay close. Putting rusty spurs to his horse's flank, he went forward at an easy walk. Bear was just able to remain by his side, while Troth and I kept apace. Right behind us came another horseman. The third horseman trotted in tandem. The rest of the soldiers, following, were strung out in a ragged line, the ox-cart coming last. Though no one said as much, we were so hemmed in we might as well have been called prisoners.

At first Dudley asked Bear about his soldiering days, which to my surprise, Bear was willing to recount at length. These were stories I had not heard before. Hard and brutal, even shocking, it was as if Bear were trying to impress the man. It greatly troubled me that Bear would invent such tales, so as to pretend he was what he wasn't.

At one point, Dudley asked Bear, "And what weapon did you fight with?"

"In those days, a sword."

"It can be so again," said Dudley. "Our cart has enough."

Bear only said, "How did you come here?"

"With the Duke of Lancaster," said Dudley. "Unlike his brother, the duke's a hateful villain. A poisonous traitor. A spawn of Satan. He's given what's English to the French, then abandoned us. Kings and princes may make wars, Master Bear, but their subjects fight them. I never signed the truce. Well then, so be it!"

"I've little love for the duke," agreed Bear.

"Then you may have an interest in where we are going," said Dudley.

"If you wish to tell me," returned Bear.

"To a bastide I know well," said Dudley. "And by my faith, a curious one."

I had no idea what a *bastide* was, but since Bear made no response, I merely listened.

"It's called Bources," said Dudley. "Do you know it?"

Bear shook his head.

"It's a village laid down—God's truth—in a perfect circle. With a castle built long ago by our own King Edward. A river moat goes round the entire town. Nothing remarkable in that, save that Bources is small, with an undersized garrison. Most curious of all, the church sits just beyond that river moat."

Bear merely nodded.

"In this church—as I have reason to know," Dudley went on, "sits a treasure chest. Graciously left by King Edward to pay for his soldiers and the church. Well then, *we* are soldiers, are we not? I mean to have it."

"By Saint Martin of Tours," said Bear after a moment, "I have no great love for priests, but to steal from a church—"

"You'll do nothing to stain your faith," said Dudley. "Your girl can do the honors."

A startled Troth looked around. I also turned, but while I had no idea what Dudley meant—even as I urgently wanted to know—I dared not speak. I glanced at Bear, but he would not return my questioning look. Instead, he tried to gain more knowledge, but Richard Dudley provided nothing more. He said, "Master Bear, it would be better for you to join us willingly. But one way or another, your ugly daughter will take part." That said, he spurred his horse and trotted on ahead. When he did so, the other two horsemen pressed in close. There was to be no escaping.

Troth's trembling hand reached out to me. I squeezed it back.

We continued on—no one speaking—but soon turned away from cliff and coast, and headed inland. We followed no road—but what seemed more like a path. The pace was slow and under the warm sun, almost pleasing. The green land became hilly, with scattered clumps of trees. Now and again, we passed a stream. We saw no other people. Once, twice, we went by what must have been houses—save that they had been destroyed. One had been tumbled, the other burned. I thought of Rye. Who, I wondered, had done *this* destruction? I recalled what Bear had once said of France, that it was full of wars—"Satan's playing fields." And here we were, marching with soldiers intent upon a *private* war, and who demanded we take part.

For the rest of the day, we went on without exchanging further words with the captain. At some point, we came upon a well-marked road and began to follow that. Bear marched along with slow steps and deep breaths. Now and again, he grunted so that I could see he had yet to recover from the voyage.

Twice we paused at small streams where the men and horses drank. Their cook—a small, skinny, and older man hardly bigger than I, with beaky nose and squinty eyes, who watched us with great interest, passed bread about, and we received a share. Ravenous, I bolted it. I had not eaten in three days.

I wanted to ask Bear many questions, but when I managed one, he only reached out and tousled my head—as much as to say, "Not yet."

That night, the captain chose to make his camp atop a hill shielded by a cap of trees. The soldiers lay about a central fire. The cook brought round a large three-legged pot and set it upon a flame. Water was fetched from a nearby stream. Dried meat, cabbage, onions, and barley— taken from the cart—were thrown in. While the cooking smells made my mouth water, my stomach spoke its appetite.

We three sat among the soldiers, for it was clear they wished us enclosed. They asked Bear about the Black Prince and his campaigns. Once again, he was nothing loath to entertain them with his tales: accounts of bloody battle and slaughter.

I listened again in stunned surprise, for he told his harsh stories with much delight and laughter. I began to wonder: were *these* things that Bear had actually done? The things he needed to confess? That he would not speak to me? I could not believe it was the Bear I knew.

Then at one point, Richard Dudley called out, "Master Bear! You claim you are a juggler! Entertain us!"

Only then did I recall that we had lost Bear's recorder— washed over during the storm. After hesitating momentarily, Bear stood up, called for some stones, and then, by the light of the flames, proceeded to juggle. The men who looked on were amused, but Bear was hardly his best. Laboring hard, he twice missed the stones. Oaflike. I was embarrassed for him. When he sat down, he was panting heavily. And he would not look at me.

I thought—with a pang—how not only had Bear's possessions been stripped away, but he had also lost his bulk, his health, and as I began to think, his dignity. When I shifted about, I saw that Troth's eyes were fixed on Bear, too. Her look was full of pain.

Before we were allowed to sleep, Dudley made sure we knew he'd posted sentries all around—no doubt meant to protect his force, but also to keep us close.

Bear set us so that we lay with our faces close, and we could talk without being overheard.

Troth put a hand to Bear's face. "There's too much warmth," she said. "Your fever has returned."

"Nothing can be done," said Bear.

"But, Bear—" I began.

"Crispin," snapped Bear, "don't waste words!"

I felt abashed.

No one spoke until Troth whispered, "What does that soldier want of me?"

"I don't know," said Bear.

"Will it be dangerous?" I said.

"I swear," said Bear, "as I live and breathe, no harm shall come to either of you."

"Bear," I asked, "what's a bastide?"

"A small market town," he said, "that's meant to defend itself. With walls perhaps, or some kind of fortification. The English and French kings built them to defend this land from Christian heretics as well as against each other."

"Bear," I asked cautiously, "those stories of war you told—they were fanciful, weren't they? You were only trying to win their sympathy . . . weren't you?"

Avoiding my look and questions, all he said was, "The both of you need your sleep."

"You didn't an—"

"Crispin," he growled, "we're in need of rest," and rolled so that his back was toward me.

I lay down. Through a break in the trees overhead I gazed upon the multitude of stars above. When I heard Bear begin his quiet snore, I twisted round and put my face close to Troth.

"Troth, do you think he really did those things?"

"I don't know."

"Are you fearful?" I asked her.

"Yes."

"I am too," I said. "I'm not sure Bear can protect us."

She didn't respond.

I looked upward again. "Troth," I said, "can you read the stars to tell the future?"

"I don't wish to."

"Why?"

"It's too hard."

Whether she meant it was too hard to see the future, or too hard to accept what she saw, I was afraid to ask.

3 2

WE SET out the next day at dawn. Beneath low clouds, the sky was layered bloodred, the air damp enough to promise rain. Richard Dudley led the way on his horse. The other soldiers marched behind, Bear, Troth, and I among them.

At one point, Dudley wheeled about and came back to speak a few words to Bear. I did not hear them. When I asked Bear what was said, he would only shake his head. His look, however, was grim enough to fill me with foreboding.

We went on. Our pace was moderate, for which I was grateful since Bear seemed weaker. He had begun to limp again and clutch the old wound. All I could think was: we must get him free.

Midmorning, a chill rain began to fall. Sometimes heavy, it turned the road and us muddy. A few times the oxcart bogged down and needed pushing and pulling to keep it going.

The farther we went, the more somber the men grew.

"Bear," I said, "what's going to happen?"

"You'll see soon enough," he said.

It was afternoon—the rain had become a gray drizzle—when we emerged from a small thicket of trees and paused. Dudley cantered back to Bear.

"The village I told you about this morning is just ahead," he said. "We'll get provisions there. Do you still not wish to take part? You can show off your sword skills."

Bear shook his head.

"But you will watch," said Dudley. "Next time—that's the important one—you'll have no choice. Is that understood?"

When Bear only nodded, Dudley galloped off.

"Bear—" I said, "you must tell us what's going to happen."

"They are going to attack a village."

"Attack!" I cried.

"And loot it."

Troth, not knowing the word, said, "What's *loot*?"

"To steal."

"Does some enemy of theirs live there?" she asked.

"Their enemy is whoever they choose to call such," said Bear.

The soldiers gathered round the oxcart. From beneath its canvas cover, they took up body armor and helmets. There were mostly dull and rusty pieces, battle-battered. Broadswords were hefted, shields gripped. Five of the men, archers, filled their quivers with arrows.

It did not take long for the men to ready themselves. A rough, ragged, and motley lot, they bristled like hedgehogs with their weaponry. Though sullen, many knelt and offered up reverent prayers and crossed themselves. Richard Dudley did the same.

When their observances were complete—marked by Dudley's standing and putting on his helmet—they moved out from beneath the cover of the trees. It was then I noticed that one of the men—armed with a sword—had been posted to guard us closely.

We moved with the others until I saw the village they were about to strike. It consisted of some fifteen small stone houses on a hillside, set so close together I was reminded of a flock of huddled sheep. Tilled fields lay below on flat land.

The houses, built of russet stone, had large wooden doors braced with iron fittings. Roofs were of red tile. Windows were small, without covering. I think I saw a little church. The air was gray, the fields dull green.

Though drizzling, perhaps fifteen people—men, women, and children—were in the field before the village. They looked no different from English peasants: boots, brown tunics, caps of muted color. One man was using an ox to break the soil with a wheeled plow. The rest were also working the earth with steady thrusts of spades. I might as well have been in my own English home.

We three were ordered to remain where we were— behind the soldiers—and observe. Our guard stood closest to Troth—as if she were the prize.

Before us, the muddy soldiers were drawn up in a long line. Led by Dudley, they began to move forward. As they did, a cock crowed. I shivered with fright.

There was nothing forceful or rushed in the soldiers' forward advance. Instead, they moved with a severe steadiness that bespoke their harrowing intent. In the center of the line came the five archers, bows in hand, each with an arrow nocked.

"Bear!" I said, "They are—"

"Be quiet!" snapped our guard.

"God have mercy," whispered Bear, and made the sign of the cross. Troth started to cover her eyes, but was so transfixed she did not do so.

The soldiers were no more than a hundred yards from the village when one of the field women stood to stretch her back. In so doing, she happened to glance round. Seeing the soldiers coming, she let out a shriek, hoisted her tunic, and ran. Startled, the other villagers looked up. Tools were dropped or flung away. The ox was abandoned. The peasants scrambled toward their houses.

Drawing bowstrings to their ears, the archers loosed their arrows. I watched—amazed—as each archer sent off some ten arrows in almost no time at all. The arrows flew in great, high arcs with a thin, *hishing* sound—only to plunge with terrible speed. Five people fell.

Even as they dropped, Richard Dudley raised his sword. He and the two horsemen galloped forward. The other soldiers—save the cook and the one who guarded us—dashed forward, swords in hand, bellowing as they went. Anyone who stood in their way was struck down.

Terrified people burst from houses, trying to escape. A few attempted to stand firm with sticks or rods. One or two had swords. I think I saw a priest. I heard a bell clang. But the resistance lasted no more than moments. All were overwhelmed. My own eyes saw some two dozen killed, mostly men, but a few women. At least two children. The priest as well.

I sank to my knees, horrified. Troth began to cry. Bear swore mightily.

Our guard laughed.

There was more. As I looked on, the soldiers began kicking doors open, moving in and out of houses, taking what they chose. They met no opposition. Mostly they took food and drink. There were too, or so I heard, a few coins stolen, perhaps some weapons. The plunder was heaped into the cart that the cook had guided to the village center to receive the goods.

Butchery and looting complete, Dudley and his free company marched off, leaving the living to bemoan their fate. As they trudged along the muddy road, the soldiers talked brightly, boasting with mirth of their martial deeds, their faces streaked with helmet rust and blood. Wine was drunk. Some men staggered. A stolen ox, tethered to the cart, was led along. Once, twice, he bellowed.

I hardly knew what to think or say. The high spirits of the soldiers brought me the deepest pain. Bear spoke not at all. Troth, by my side, now and again took my hand. That hand was cold, and trembled.

I turned to Bear more than once. All I could ask was, "Why?"

"We'll talk later," he muttered and cast a darting glance at the men around us by way of warning. I said no more.

But Heaven—with its gentle, if unceasing rain—wept.

33

HAT NIGHT, after camp was set atop a small hill—their usual defensive practice— the soldiers made merry. They drank much and sang harsh songs. Dudley joined them. At one point, he staggered up to us—for we sat glumly apart—and, pointing right at Troth, shouted, "Tomorrow, ugly one, you'll be there with us!"

As he stumbled away, Bear reached out and drew Troth to his chest. She pulled away and sat rigidly, fingering her hawthorn sprig, staring I knew not where. Though not said, we understood the need to wait until we could talk privately.

Gradually, the soldiers succumbed to sleep. Such light as there was came from the dwindling central fire. I could just see Bear's face—wan, full of sorrow. Troth's visage—pale, tense.

"Bear," I whispered, "you must talk to us."

He shook his great head. "God's truth! What can I tell you that you don't already know?"

"Why did these men do such a thing?"

He took a deep breath. "Earlier this year, the Duke of Lancaster—he for King Edward—and the Frenchman, Bernard Du Guesclin—he for his King Charles—made a truce. Which is to say, yet another pause in this never-ending war. As usually happens, there are dismissed soldiers with nowhere to go. Answering to no lord, they do as they choose, plundering as they wish. Free companies, they're called. Though they may send their prayers to our Jesus, they're no better than those who killed Him. Brigands. Murderers."

He became silent.

In that silence, I said, "Bear, those stories you told Dudley, about those things you said you did when a soldier. You . . . were you making them up . . . weren't you . . . to gain their trust?"

Bear looked at me, eyes full of pain. He started to speak, stopped, took a deep breath and spoke most haltingly. "Crispin," he said, "on Judgment Day . . . when . . .

when all shall kneel to be judged before our Blessed Lord, no man who has warred shall be unblemished."

Stunned by what he was saying, I was afraid to speak. My eyes filled with tears.

Bear reached out, touched my cheek and whispered, "A child's tear is the true holy water."

I could not speak.

"Listen well," said Bear, recovering some strength in his voice. "Both of you. Most of my days I lived for myself. I was free. I was a sinner, like these men, but, as God knows, not all I did was bad. But much was. Then you two came. Crispin first. Then Troth. In the full measure of my life, it's not been for so very long. I can only pray that God will say it's enough. To find such love as I have for both of you is to bind oneself to life, and living. And as my Lord Jesus knows and teaches—a new, and loving life cleanses the old."

"And you *are* kind!" I cried.

"And good!" added Troth.

"I pray that God may forgive me as generously as you two do!" said Bear. Impulsively, he reached out and hugged us to his chest. "It's you," he whispered, "who are my redemption. In children there is mercy."

"Bear—" I said.

"Crispin, I am tired to my soul. More than tired."

"What do you mean?" I cried.

"I must rest. To find some place and stay. I've wandered too much. My sins hold me back so that I can hardly move."

Then Troth, very softly, asked, "What will happen tomorrow?"

"Richard Dudley means to attack the village of which he spoke. You heard him: he claims a fortune is to be found there. He insists that in you, Troth—being small and agile—he's found a way to reach it. Exactly how, I don't know. But I will make every effort to ensure you're safe."

"We should run off now," I said.

Bear shook his head. "Crispin, by our Blessed Lady, we cannot. They are watching us. If we try to escape, we'll be cut down. Or at least you and I. They mean to use Troth. We need to be here for her. We'll know more tomorrow. Let's hope all goes well."

I said, "You once told me a wise man has as many hopes as reasons. Is that all that's left to you—hope?"

He sighed. I studied Bear's face. He *had* become old.

He reached out and chucked me on the chin. "Yes, hope."

"Hope for what?" I cried.

"That we do not," he whispered, "fail each other."

34

AWN CAME with gray skies, the air sweet and soft, holding hints of more rain. The trees upon the hill where we camped, stirred in a gentle breeze. Birds flew high and in haste, as if—I thought—to escape. How I wished we had such wings! How I dreaded the coming day!

The cook broke our fast with bowls of mashed wheat grain. We ate with our fingers. The soldiers, stiff and slow to rise, put themselves into battle garb. After their night of revelry, they were sober in mind and spirit again. Some, as before, went on their knees in prayer.

What kind of men—I wondered—were these that killed by day, drank by night, but prayed each morning?

Richard Dudley did not deign to speak to us. Instead, he urged his men to complete their preparations. Only when that was done, did he mount his horse and lead the way from the encampment. As before, we three were herded among the rest and made to march along. Bear limped and offered no talk. It caused me grief to see him so resigned. If ever there was a time, I told myself, now I must be a man. But even as I had the thought, I made a correction: no, I thought, be just yourself and find a way to free Bear and Troth.

Toward midday, we worked our way just behind the forested crest of another hill. It was there, among some trees, partly hidden, that Dudley called a halt. He ordered his troops to stay back. No fire could be made lest it give off smoke.

He came to us. "Follow me," he commanded.

We went to one side of the hill, standing among some trees from where we were able to gaze out upon a flat plain. Dudley drew Troth to him roughly and made her stand before him, putting his thick hands on her shoulders so she could not bolt. That he even touched her filled me with rage.

Bear and I stood to either side—as close as we dared.

What we saw was a sweet, green valley, tilled fields, occasional trees, a pond or two, plus a serpentine river that ran through all. People were at work in the fields. Near the center of this unruffled world stood a circle of a village with some fifty structures set about a tree-filled center. No wall around it. Instead, the river flowed toward it, and then went completely around it—thus serving as a wide moat that provided protection.

A drawbridge crossed the water. At the point where this bridge crossed, a castle stood within. Built of dark gray stone, it was some four levels high, longer than wide, with a crenellated rampart. At the end nearest the river moat, a round keep had been built. It had a fair number of arrow slits from which archers could shoot down to defend the bridge. Here and there, a corbel had been built for the same purpose. The keep's top rampart was also crenellated. From it hung a flag.

"That," said Richard Dudley, "is Bourses. And *there* is our treasure." He swung about, and pointed to a large church built of the same gray stone as the castle. But the church stood *outside* the moat.

At first glance, the church looked no different from other churches I had seen. Longer than it was wide, it had extensions to either side to give it the shape of a cross. The main entry—large double wooden doors—was at the side rather than at the front of the church. A cross stood above it.

But here, one end of the church abutted the river. At the other end was a tower—part of the church, but not a spire. The high cross was elsewhere. This tower was a tall, square structure with a pointed roof. From what I could see, its entryway must have been *within* the church. Moreover, the upper part of this tower had slits from which one might shoot arrows down. In short, it was something I had never seen before: a fortified church. In so being, it also guarded the drawbridge that crossed the river.

"King Edward," said Dudley with a grin, "decreed that the church, not the garrison, should protect the treasure. Which is to say, he trusted his priests more than his officers."

"How do you intend to get at it?" asked Bear.

"A deception," said Dudley. "Most of the soldiers are in that castle," he said. "The flag proclaims as much. My men and I shall act as if we intend to attack it, that we are laying on a siege. That will keep all forces within the castle, as well as draw those who are stationed in the church. That will leave the church unguarded—save a few. Of course it will be closed. But happily, there is a opening at the base of the tower. Can you see it?"

We looked. I could see a small hole near the base of the fortified tower.

"Why is it there?" asked Dudley. "Well now, do you see how the church is set up against the river moat? At times the river rises and floods. That water floods the church. But those holes—and at the other end—allow the water to flow out.

"The river-end hole sits beneath the waterline. And the land-side hole is too small for any grown man. But it's not," he said, slapping his hands hard down on Troth's shoulders, "too small for this unhappy girl.

"Very well then, my ugly one," he went on. "You shall go through the opening, slip inside, thereby gaining access to the church. Once within, you'll open the doors. We shall be waiting and watching. The moment we see the doors swing out, my troops and I shall wheel about, enter the church, and pluck up the treasure."

"How are the doors kept closed?" Bear asked.

"A wooden crossbeam. On the inside. Is she strong?" Dudley asked.

"Strong enough," said Bear. Then he asked, "Will there not be soldiers inside the church?"

Dudley shrugged. "At most, the few who barred the door from within. It shall be the girl's task to get by them."

"And if she cannot?"

"We'll try again. With your boy. With two chances, we should succeed."

Bear struggled for words. "Whose soldiers are in the castle?"

"The flag tells us it's an English garrison."

"Then you're attacking your own people," said Bear.

"They would as soon slay me."

"Is it not King Edward's wealth?"

"You said he died. Well, then, I proclaim it forfeit."

We stared silently at the view before us.

"When do you intend to do this?"

"Right now. Before we're discovered. Very well: I have instructed the girl what to do. Have I been clear? Answer me!"

"Yes," said Troth.

"What did she say?" demanded Dudley. "I can't understand her."

"She said yes," said Bear.

"Then she spoke well! Now then," he said to Bear, "you will be with me while we attack the castle—even as she enters the church."

"And the boy?"

"He will remain behind—with the cook. If the girl fails, we'll use him to do the job. What say you, boy?"

"Bear's not strong enough," I said. "Let me go in his place."

"Absolutely not," said Bear quickly.

"But—"

"Crispin!" cried Bear. "Do as he says."

I stared at him, hardly knowing what to think or

feel: furious about what was happening, angry that he was still trying to protect me, afraid that I was being left alone, frustrated that I would not be able to do anything.

Dudley, however, only smiled. "So be it," he said.

"Now, tell me . . . what will happen to me?" said Bear. He was struggling to contain his anger.

"As I said, you shall stay by my side," said Dudley. "With a halter round your neck. To keep you from escaping."

"A halter!" I cried.

"Shhh!" said Bear. "Will I be armed?"

"I think not," said Dudley with something of a smile. "You might attack me. No, you shall be held hostage until the girl—or boy—achieves what I desire. So then, girl, boy, hear me well: if you do *not* succeed in the task I've set you, I'll slay your father. Is that understood? The treasure in the church is his ransom. Which is to say, it's on you whether he lives or dies. Help me get the treasure, and you shall all be freed. Fail, and his life—and yours—are forfeit. Is that clearly understood?"

Troth could only nod. I suppose I did too.

Dudley turned to Bear. "Now, get yourself some armor."

35

HE THREE of us walked slowly back to the oxcart. Right behind came an armed guard.

"Bear—" I began.

"Let me think!" he barked, cutting me off.

"Troth can't do such a thing," I persisted.

"Crispin," said Troth, "I'll do what he asked. Then he'll set us free."

"I don't think he will," I cried to her. "And what if Bear is hurt or killed in the attack? Didn't you hear? He'll have a halter tied round his neck! He won't even be armed."

Troth said nothing to that.

"Do *you* trust Dudley to set us free, if he gets his treasure?" I demanded of Bear.

"By Saint Jerome, I don't know," was Bear's reply. We had reached the oxcart. Under the watchful eye of both the guard and the cook, Bear leaned into the oxcart and searched about for a piece of armor that might fit him.

He fetched up a chain mail shirt. It was corroded, and had some holes. Nonetheless, he pulled it over his head so that it covered half his arms, his neck, and most of his chest.

Troth and I looked on glumly.

Next, Bear rummaged around the oxcart for a breast-plate. When he found one, he held it to his body for a fitting, knocking it with his knuckles to see if it was sound.

"Crispin," he said. "Help me with the straps."

I had watched his dressing with mounting despair. "Bear, we can get away and—"

"Crispin," he barked, "remember: the man who thinks his enemy is a fool, is the greater fool. Now do as I say!"

Troth watched, wide-eyed as I, fumbling, buckled the leather straps behind Bear's back so the plate was held to his chest. It fit poorly.

Bear next took up a helmet—examined it indifferently—and set it on his head.

He turned to the guard. "There are swords in there," he said, with a nod to the cart. "Can I arm myself?"

"No," said the man. "You heard the captain."

Bear shrugged.

I looked at Bear. Though he did not have his old bulk, he was still a large man, but the ill-fitting plate and helmet served to make him ungainly and vulnerable in appearance.

"Now, come," said Bear, "we have just a little time." He put his arm about my shoulder, did as much with Troth, and began to draw us away.

The cook called, "The boy is to stay here!" He held up a sword of his own to show his strength.

"In good faith, I'll have him for just a moment," Bear called back. "You may watch us! I wish to make sure they know what to do."

The cook lowered his sword. "Be quick," he said.

With us at his side, Bear set his steps toward where Dudley waited with his troops. Halfway there, Bear stopped. No one was around us. "Listen well," he said, his voice hushed but urgent. "We have this last moment."

"Bear . . ." I began.

He touched my mouth to keep me still, then placed a large hand on each our shoulders and bent close so that our three heads were touching. "Know the love I have for you both," he began. "As God is holy, you must escape, and find your way to freedom. You'll most likely have to do so without me."

Seething with frustration, I wanted to speak but could not.

He went on: "Know there is nothing in this that you have done. You are both without sin."

I felt like screaming at him, hitting him with my rage that he was not letting me do *anything*, but insisting—as he did of old—to tell me what to do, refusing to allow me to act as I might. "Bear—"

"Crispin," he hissed, "don't argue! Now, I will go along with Captain Dudley, and see what God has in store. Troth, start off as he bid you. Crispin, you *must* free yourself from the one who guards you. Join Troth. It's your only hope. As soon as you meet, run off. The two of you need each other."

"But what of you?" I cried.

"By my Blessed Lady, I have no desire to leave off living," he said. "But if you two can free yourselves, my prayers will be answered. Perhaps God has some means for us to stay together. If He does, I don't know it."

"Bear," I pleaded, "you must let me—"

"Crispin, honor me and my love by living free. Troth, do the same. Cling to one another. Find some place to be. Let it be as it *may* be! Pray for my soul, but never neglect your own. Do you understand me, Crispin? Free yourself and get to Troth. Do what you must do. Is that clear?"

"Yes, but—"

Bear, breathing heavily, would not stop, would not let me say one thing. "Troth," he went on, "trust yourself first, then Crispin. Always honor Aude. Find a way to live that lets you be yourself. No God—yours or mine—can ask for more."

That said, he reached round and pulled us toward him in an embrace.

I could not—would not— believe it would be our last.

Bear turned sharply away from me. Guiding Troth with a large hand at her back, they went where Dudley waited with his soldiers. Bear was followed by the guard.

My heart a burning stone in my chest, I remained behind, watching them go. Twice Bear looked back at me over his shoulder. So did Troth. She made a quick hand sign: *come*. I would have bolted that instant, if I had not felt a sharp poke upon my back. I turned. It was the little cook. His sword was in his hand.

"You're to come with me," he commanded.

Which was greater, my despair or my rage, I can hardly say. I only know that I was trembling, my vision blurry. I had to struggle to find breath.

I allowed myself one last look at Bear and Troth, and then let myself be guided back to the cart. As we went, I strained to find some degree of self-possession, knowing I must think clearly, grasping that my task was to get free quickly. I had little doubt I would have but one chance—if that.

Once at the oxcart, the cook pulled up a coil of rope,

one end of which had already been tied to the spoke of the cartwheel. The cook fastened the other end round one of my arms, pulling the knot taut.

"By Saint Peter," he said as he tethered me, "small as I am, Captain Dudley had marked me to be the one to go into that tower. But God answered my prayers when you came along with that wretched girl. A good captain, if a hard man. For your own sake, you'd best pray she'll succeed. For now, lad, rest easy. There's nothing you can do." That said, he busied himself among his iron pots, content to let me be his prisoner.

I stood there, trying to shape my fury, using it to make a plan. From where I was, I could see the troops, plus Dudley and two others on horseback. Bear, large as he was, stood out from the others. I watched, horrified, as a soldier slung a rope round his neck, and pulled it tight like a hanging noose. Even as I had been tied to the oxcart, Bear was tied to the pommel of Dudley's saddle.

I could no longer see Troth. But as sure as I knew anything, I had no doubt she would not run away as Bear bade her. To try and save him, she would do as Dudley had commanded.

The soldiers were forming up, receiving final instructions from Dudley.

"Will the captain keep his word?" I called to the cook.

He looked up from his pot, into which he was cutting onions with his dagger. "It depends on what happens," he said, wiping his eyes. "Captain Dudley has talked of that treasure for many a month. God willing, he'll have it. And I beg your forgiveness in advance, but I've been ordered to slay you"—he nodded to his sword which lay close to his hand—"if you act ill. Pay heed: my life is forfeit if I disobey the captain."

He spoke with ease. That he meant to act by his orders, I had little doubt. He had his sword, and there was a dagger in his hand. I had nothing.

I swung back round to watch the troops. They had begun to move off the hill, presumably toward the castle. The last I saw of Bear, he was being led away like a captive beast.

36

 HAT I DID FIRST—with my back to the cook—was pluck at the knot that held me. But it was too tightly drawn, and when I glanced round at the cook and found his eyes on me, I left off.

Baffled, I slumped against the cart and racked my brains for something else to do. It was then that I recalled Bear's words: he had turned to the guard and said, "There are swords in there," and nodded toward the cart.

Belatedly, I realized he had been talking to *me!* He had told me where I might find a sword.

Heart pounding, I measured with my eye the rope that held me, as well as the height of the cart. I decided the rope was—hopefully—long enough to let me reach into the cart.

I glanced at the cook. For the moment he was turned away from me, dagger in his belt, tearing at some cabbage leaves. "Saint Giles, be with me," I whispered. Fully aware that I would have but one chance, I made a hasty sign of the cross.

I took a deep breath, set one foot on a wheel spoke, then hastily heaved myself up. My leap was barely high enough to allow me to bend into the cart. Sure enough I saw a sword—had Bear moved it closer? I reached for it. In my haste, not only did I miss, I tipped it away. Frantic, I lunged a second time. That effort allowed me to snatch the hilt. Grasping it tightly, I swung it around in a wide arch, while leaping back, so that I landed awkwardly on my feet.

The cook heard me. Startled, he turned about. Seeing what I'd done, he gawked for a moment. In that brief time,

I pulled the rope that bound me tight, swung the sword down, and chopped at it with all my strength. It split apart.

I was free.

But now the cook snatched up his sword and leaped toward me.

I was no swordsman, much less a fighter. I could only do such things as Bear had tried to teach me. What's more, no matter the cook's intent, I had no desire of harming the little man. Escape was all.

Yet the cook would have at me, swinging wildly with his sword, swearing vile oaths, vowing he would kill me. But as God was kind, I found myself quick enough to parry his efforts with my sword. When he fell back, ready to strike again, I grasped the handle of my sword in both hands and swung out at him as hard as I was able. Even as I did, he also struck so that our swords met with an ear-breaking *clang* of metal. The force of my blow caught him unprepared. His sword was knocked entirely out of his hands, where it fell some paces away.

Red-faced with rage, he gave not an inch but snatched up his dagger and came at me furiously. I retreated, holding the sword before me. "Get back!" I screamed.

Trying to outwit me, he sidestepped, and then, with dagger raised and poised to strike, he threw himself at me.

In hasty defense, I swung round, lifted my sword toward him—so that he ran himself upon it.

He hung there, openmouthed, in skewered surprise.

Terrified by what I'd done, I jumped back, bloody sword in hand, and stood there as he fell to his knees, blood gushing from his wound and mouth. Eyes rolling, he mouthed some garbled words—might they have been holy prayers!—then fell forward, face into the earth.

Horrified, my stomach heaving, so dizzy with fright I could hardly stand, I was compelled to lean upon the nearby wagon. "Forgive me, forgive me . . ." I murmured, and though I tried to make the sign of the cross, my hand shook so I could not.

I waited one more dreadful moment, gulping for air, afraid to look at the dead man. Then I recalled myself, turned, and ran, the death-dripping sword still in hand.

Trying not to think of what had just happened, I charged to the crest of the hill where we had stood before and looked down at the round village of Bources. The view was much the same, and yet in process of much alteration.

Dudley and his men were marching in a line toward the castle, banneret fluttering. They were going very slowly, deliberately, even slower than when they attacked the village.

I looked for Bear, and saw him easily enough, he being

larger than the rest. He was close to Dudley, held by the rope that kept him a hostage to Troth's success.

At first I was puzzled by the soldier's slow advance. Then I realized it was only what Dudley had schemed—to show himself and his force, thereby bringing all the opposition garrison to the castle, away from the church.

Sure enough, I could see considerable movement on the castle ramparts. Soldiers were rushing about behind the crenellation. Horns were being blown, bleating shrill alarms. A bell began to sound.

The peasants in the field stopped, listened, and began to run toward the village.

I turned toward the church and the fortified tower. The church doors swung open. A body of soldiers and a priest burst out. From the way their faces were set, I could see they were looking toward Dudley and his men. Even as I watched, the priest and the soldiers raced across the drawbridge— going, I presumed, to defend and be protected by the castle. As soon as they passed, the drawbridge lifted. Not all the soldiers went. A few returned to the church. The doors shut.

It was all as Dudley had planned.

But were there more soldiers within the church? How many would there be for Troth to contend with?

Trying to keep from panicking, I gazed about but did

not see her. I had no doubt, however, she was heading for that tower hole.

Sword in hand, I ran down the hill, straight for the tower. I had taken no more than a few steps when I realized I must take pains not to be seen. Not by Dudley's men. Nor by anyone in the church. If I were seen by anyone, Bear's life would be forfeit.

Crouched but still running, I ran forward in a great circle, away from Dudley's force but hoping to come upon the tower indirectly. Now and again, I bobbed up in hopes of seeing Troth. But even when I came within fifty yards of the church tower, I had no idea where she was.

Meanwhile, Dudley and his men were now opposite the castle, keeping to the far side of the moat. His archers were shooting arrows. Though I was sure Dudley would make no attempt to cross the moat, those within the castle could not know that. I saw archers atop the castle ramparts lean forward and loose their arrows at the attackers. And Bear without a shield!

Knowing I had to find Troth, I forced myself to take my eye from the castle and look at the church tower. First, I took note of the flow hole that Dudley had spoken of, the one that he told Troth she must use to gain entry to the tower. I found it easily enough. I also caught sight of some movement aloft, behind the tower archer holes. That meant that some of the soldiers I had seen—still impossible to know how many—were within, ready to defend the treasure. The more there were, the more danger for Troth.

Taking a chance, I stood up, looked about. This time I saw her. She'd done as I had expected, gone to the tower, albeit indirectly, moving along the moat's embankment, trying to reach the tower walls without being seen.

Wanting to reach her before she went any farther, I dashed around—as she must have done—toward the river moat. I knew I might be observed from the far side of the moat, but felt I had no choice.

I reached the embankment safely, and dropped down, wanting to keep myself hidden from those within the tower.

Troth was some thirty yards before me. She appeared to be gathering herself for a run to the tower.

Ignoring caution, I shouted, "Troth!"

She paused, turned, and looked back.

"Wait!" I cried. Still bent over, I ran forward along the moat bank.

"Troth," I blurted out when I reached her, "I killed the one guarding me." I held up the sword, still stained with blood.

In revulsion, she stepped back.

"He would have killed me," I said. "Troth, he attacked me."

She gazed at me for a moment, then turned away, and looked toward the church.

"What do you wish to do?" she asked, her face averted.

"I don't care what Bear told us," I said. "We must help him."

"I thought the same," said Troth. "I've an idea."

"What?"

"I'll do what Dudley ordered. When I open the church doors—that's what he wanted—he'll lead his soldiers to the church. But, Crispin, he'll be thinking mostly of the treasure. Then that's when we must reach Bear and get him away."

"Troth, Dudley tied a rope to Bear's neck to hold him." Her mouth opened in shock.

"And not all the soldiers left the church."

"How many are there?"

"I don't know. I'm sure I saw some in the tower. Behind the arrow slits."

Troth looked up. "I'm going anyway," she said. "Stay here—in case I fail." She made a movement to go.

I held her with a hand. "We'll have a better chance to get the doors open with two of us inside."

Troth offered no argument. Instead, she turned back

to scrutinize the tower. "Crispin," she said, "if we can get against the tower and move flat along the walls, they shouldn't be able to see us, or shoot at us, before we get to that hole."

She was right: the arrow slots were some one hundred feet above the ground, designed to repel attackers at a distance. Nor were there any turrets for shooting directly down.

"But we must hurry," I agreed.

That said, she jumped up and raced for the church walls. I scrambled to follow, too fearful to look up.

37

 ITH TROTH in the lead, me following behind, we ran hard. The ground between the moat and the church being level, we reached the church walls quickly. No arrows were shot, which, I could only pray, meant that we were as yet unnoticed.

Once arrived, we pressed against the rough, stone church walls, and began to edge around. As we went, I could hear shouts, cries, and blaring horns from the castle side, but we could see nothing. I kept thinking of Bear.

We reached the base of the tower, and—as far as I knew—had still not been observed. Pushing forward, we came to the hole.

Once there, while trying to regain our breath, we squatted down and studied what to do.

The hole was some two feet wide, perhaps two in height. That is, large enough for us to pass through, as long at it became no smaller within. But when I squatted down to look inside, I found the hole blocked. With Troth looking over my shoulder, I used my sword to poke about.

To my relief, I found that the hole was stuffed with little more than leaves and silt. Working hard with my sword and hands, I was able to scoop it clear to some depth.

"I'll go first," I said. "I'll tell you if it's safe."

"And if it isn't?"

"You must flee," I said, and before she could return an answer, I handed her my sword, and plunged headfirst into the hole, arms first to feel my way, my feet kicking me forward.

It was dim within the hole. The stone surrounding me was hard, rough, and cold. Such light as there was seeped in from behind. Happily, the farther in I went, the more the hole widened. As I slithered forward in snakelike fashion, I came upon more dirt, which I was able to push behind me, even as I wriggled on.

I pressed forward for what must have been some five feet—the thickness of the tower wall. Before me I saw dim light. Just when I thought I was clear, my fingers, which I had extended as far out as I could reach, touched metal.

It was too dark to see what it was, but when I worked my fingers about, it felt as if crossed bars had been set across the inside opening as a kind of net. I squeezed forward, grasped the bars with my one free hand, and shook them. The bars were somewhat loose, perhaps rusted from water flow. Encouraged, I rattled them with greater violence. The bars gave way, falling in with a clatter.

Kicking and pulling, I eased out of the hole. Once free, I stood on the stone floor and glanced about. The room was square, stone-walled, suffused by dim light, which seeped down from a stairwell in one corner. Circular steps led upward.

At the other side of the room was a large door fitted with elaborate iron fastenings, including a handle. Near the door's base were holes, perhaps for the flow of water. There was nothing else.

On my knees I called to Troth through the hole. "Come through," I called.

"Take the sword first," she called.

Within moments, I had the sword, and Troth was with

me. She wasted no time, but went directly to the wooden door and jerked the handle. The door would not budge.

"We can try that way," I whispered, nodding toward the steps.

The narrow steps wound tightly upward. As we climbed—I first, with sword in hand—we pressed against the cold, inner wall. After some forty-or-so high steps, we reached a new level and another door, a small one. We paused to listen. From the stairwell above we could hear sounds, even excited voices, but we could not make out the words.

Troth went to the small door and shoved. It creaked open. Cautiously, she pushed it further, then peeked out. She made a hand gesture that I understood to mean *safe*, then passed on through the doorway.

I followed.

We found ourselves upon a narrow balcony enclosed by an iron railing. Thirty feet below us was the high altar, upon which stood a stone cross. To the right of that, a baptismal font. Above us, a stained glass window, rich in blues and reds. Before us, the stone-paved nave opened out. As far as we could see, all was deserted.

We could also see the principal doorway to the church—the one we were supposed to open—off to one side at the far end, quite opposite where we stood. I took note of the wooden crossbeam that kept it closed. It was large, and from the look of it, heavy.

I also saw an alcove midway along the length of the church's nave. A Lady chapel perhaps. And, in the very middle of the nave, a low stone platform, upon which a chest had been placed. The chest was wrapped about with chains. I had no doubt. It was that for which Dudley lusted: King Edward's treasure.

I leaned over the railing. Below us I could see a door in the wall, near the baptismal font. I supposed it to be the door we could not open.

But the narrow balcony—upon which we stood and which ran round the altar—had a ladder at its farthest end. Built into the wall, it reached the church floor. Since we needed to get down to the nave, we'd have to use it.

I nudged Troth and pointed to the ladder.

Halfway to the ladder, we heard a great bang, followed by agitated voices. Not knowing where the noise was coming from, we stopped. A glance at the church's front entryway revealed nothing. When the voices grew louder, I guessed they were coming from the tower door. Sure enough, the next moment we saw two soldiers—one old, the other young—run the span of the nave below. One was armed with a sword.

In haste, we threw ourselves flat upon the balcony floor so as to be unnoticed. But we could see the soldiers go to the main door. At first I thought they meant to open it. It appeared, however, that they were only making certain it remained closed. The task done, they headed back the way they came, only to momentarily disappear from view. In quick time, one of the soldiers emerged—the older one. He ran, empty-handed, back in the direction of the tower door.

One soldier remained. And he—I realized—must have kept the sword.

Since it was clear that if we used the ladder we would be observed, we remained where we were, stymied. I made bold to lean out over the balcony, and looked back toward the door that we'd been unable to open before. What I discovered was the door had been left ajar—no doubt by the soldier we had just seen.

I reached out, touched Troth, and motioned for her to follow. We hurried back as we came, down the steps, then slipped through the open door. By so doing, we found ourselves on the floor of the church. I pointed toward the alcove where the young soldier must be praying. Troth nodded her understanding.

I darted forward and crouched behind the stone altar. Troth joined me.

"If we rush forward at the same time," I whispered, "that soldier won't be able to stop both of us. I'll engage with him while you get to the door."

"Crispin," she said, "he has a sword."

By way of answer, I held up mine. "He's young," I said. "No bigger than me."

She said, "He's a soldier."

"Troth, think of Bear. We have to hurry. Are you ready?"

She nodded.

Heart thumping, I took a deep breath, gripped my sword tightly, and sprinted loudly toward the main door. Halfway there, the soldier poked his head out from the alcove. When he saw us, the look on his face was one of surprise. It lasted only a moment. Sword in hand, he jumped out in front of us. "I . . . I command you to stop!" he stammered.

"Troth!" I shouted. "To the door!" and placed myself between her and the soldier, my own sword raised.

The soldier made a movement toward Troth, only to stop and turn about when I shouted, "Give way!"

Sword extended, he advanced on me. He had a pale, youthful face, eyes large with fright. Unsure of himself, he was panting for breath.

Desiring to draw him from Troth, I took a step back. Even as I did—from the corner of my eye—I saw her slip past.

The soldier, grasping what we were doing, spun about, and went after Troth. She had reached the door. Her hands were on the beam, her back to the soldier.

"Troth!" I screamed.

Turning, she saw the young soldier just as he was about to bring his sword down and leaped away. The soldier swung again, violently, wildly. For a second time she managed to elude him. Rushing forward, I cried "Here!" to draw the soldier's attention. The soldier whirled about anew—as if he knew not which way to turn—to now confront me with his sword. Once more I tried to lead him away by backing up.

This time, however, knowing that our aim was to unbar the door, he did not advance but stood his ground and began to bellow to his companions, "Give aid! Give aid!"

38

 T WOULD BE, I knew, just moments before others came to help him.

Troth gestured, telling me to *advance to the side*.

I crept forward as she bid, my heavy sword in both

hands, shifting it back and forth.

The soldier, unable to watch the two of us at once, put his eyes solely on me—the sword bearer.

His face glistened with sweat. He was breathing hard. He started to step forward, only to hold back.

Knowing he was waiting for his companions, and feeling the pressure to draw him, I crept closer. Instead of holding the sword with two hands, I used just one so I could extend my reach that much further. It was enough to rub against the soldier's blade. The rough, grating sound made me clench my teeth.

Grimacing, he advanced, swinging his sword out with all his strength, albeit uncontrollably. Sensing a rash confidence on his part, I yielded a few steps, trying to act as if I were overawed. Tempted, he came forward, moving even farther from the door. When I continued to step back, he came with me like a fish drawn on a line. Now and again, our swords touched—a sharp, teasing ring.

No doubt believing he'd gained the advantage, he began to press me harder, using his sword to force me into a further retreat.

Troth—I could just see—was getting closer to the door.

The soldier pounced, and in so doing, struck my sword with so much force it was all I could do to keep it in my grasp. Sensing my weakness, he waited not at all, but struck again and again, crashing his sword hard against mine.

It was then that Troth dove forward and reached the door. Using both hands, she shoved up on one end of the crossbeam, got it over one of the iron holds, and let it drop. It fell with a crash, but it still barred the door.

The noise alarmed the soldier so, he hesitated in his attack on me. Though he still held his sword out, he darted a look back. At that instant, I gathered all my strength and swung my sword against his. In his moment of distraction, I was able to shake his hold. Desperate, I struck again. That time I hit the side of his arm. He yelped with pain. Blood began to flow. With a clatter, his sword dropped. Scrambling to pick it up, he slipped on his own blood and went down on his knees. Thinking I would surely strike, he lifted his arms over his head.

Instead, I used the moment to leap to the door where Troth was struggling to lift the other end of the crossbeam. With two of us hoisting, it rose up enough so that we could pull it free. It fell with a crash. Even as it did, we pushed against the doors.

They swung open.

Ten armed soldiers—helmeted and in body armor—

poured out of the tower door and came rushing down the length of the church nave toward us.

Side by side, Troth and I ran out of the church.

Dudley's troops must have seen the church doors swing open. By the time Troth and I burst from the building, they were already rushing toward us. Foremost, Dudley and his two lieutenants were charging on their mounts, their swords up. To my horror, I saw that Bear still had the rope round his neck and was being all but dragged forward by Dudley.

Troth and I leaped to one side just as the soldiers within the church burst out the door. When they saw what was coming at them, most rushed forward to confront the onslaught. Others raced to close the doors.

As I watched, I saw one of the church soldiers lift a crossbow and shoot at one of the advancing horsemen. The bolt struck the man with so much force he spun about and fell to the ground. His beast, in confusion, twisted about, colliding into the other horse, breaking the momentum of Dudley's attacking troops.

The fighting at the church door was as fierce as it was tangled. Shouts and screams, and the constant clang of metal on metal filled the air. Men fell. The ground was soaked with blood. Even as we searched for Bear, Troth and I tried to keep free of the fierce fighting.

"There!" screamed Troth and pointed.

I saw Bear. He was on his knees, desperately trying to get the rope from around his neck, even while attempting to keep from being hauled about. He had lost his helmet. His body plate was askew. His garments were rent in many places. Though there were soldiers around him, no one was paying attention to him. But the rope still held, and, attached to Dudley's horse, was yanked this way and that as the captain fought, utterly unmindful of what was happening to Bear.

"Stay here!" I shouted to Troth and dashed forward, sword in hand.

There were soldiers all around me, yelling and screaming. More than once I dodged a stroke from one side or another, I hardly knew which.

"Bear," I screamed so hard it hurt my throat, trying to make myself heard above the furor.

He turned toward the sound of my voice. His eyes were wide with panic, his face filthy, one cheek gashed and bleeding profusely. His red beard fairly glistened with blood.

I reached his side. "Hold out the rope!" I shouted.

When he did, I struck, severing it. He fell, free, then made an effort to get back on his feet, only to stumble.

"Take the sword!" I yelled, thrusting it in his hand. He

took it while I ducked my head beneath his arm, and strove to lift him. "Push up!" I cried. He struggled and finally rose up.

Clumsily, step-by-step, we tried to move away from the melee in the direction where I thought I had left Troth.

As I went, I shifted slightly and saw the fighting at the church. As I would understand only later, once Dudley's forces had turned to attack the church, the garrison within the castle left the fortification, crossed the lowered moat, and were now pressing Dudley and his troops from behind. Moreover, with one church door closed, the fighting had become more desperate. The howls and shrieks of pain, mixed with the constant clash of metal on metal, produced an appalling chorus of butchery.

Troth saw us, and began to run in our direction.

There was a great shout behind us. I shifted about, and saw that the second church door had been closed.

"Retreat! Retreat!" I heard from Dudley's men.

Even Bear turned his head.

Dudley's men were trying to break away from the church before they became encircled and annihilated.

Next moment, I saw Dudley, still mounted, repeatedly slashing with his sword, forcing his way through the ring of garrison troops who were trying to bring him down with spears, glaives, and swords.

Suddenly, he broke though and galloped forward. Troth was running toward us—directly in his path. Dudley, red-faced with fury, swerved straight toward her—as if to trample her.

Bear saw the danger.

"Troth!" he screamed, and broke from me with sword in hand. Stumbling as much as he ran, he hurled himself forward to block Dudley's way. The captain saw him. Instead of drawing back or away, he lifted his sword, prepared to slash Bear. It was then that Bear flung—javelinlike— his sword forward. It struck the horse in the neck. When hit, the horse jerked his head up, stumbled, and fell to its knees. The shock of the horse's collapse caused Dudley to be thrown over its head onto the ground. The horse, recovering, whinnied shrilly, shook itself to a standing position, and, though bleeding profusely from its neck, bolted.

Dudley lay facedown upon the ground, unmoving.

Bear had also fallen to his hands and knees. With enormous effort, he scrambled for his sword that lay not far from where he was upon the ground. Taking hold of it with two hands, he used it as a prop to stagger up, then lurched toward the prostrate Dudley. It was perfectly clear what he intended—to kill the fallen man.

Troth raced forward. "Bear!" she screamed. "Don't! You mustn't kill!"

Bear, his sword poised over Dudley, hesitated.

Troth came to his side. She reached up and pulled his arm down. To my amazement, Bear let her. Indeed, she took the sword from his hands and with all her strength, flung it away.

39

E LED BEAR AWAY as far from the fighting as we could. When we came to a cluster of trees thick enough to conceal us, we crept within. Once there, we lay him upon the ground.

Eyes closed, Bear was broken and battered, with more than one bleeding wound. Rope-burn marks scored his neck. We tried to clean his face of blood and filth, but we had no water.

We did not talk. All we could do was stay close, both Troth and I holding Bear's hands.

The clamor of the battle dwindled until we could hear no more. No one came to look for us. We remained alone.

Once—before it was completely dark—Bear opened his eyes. He looked at us, eyes full of tears. He tried to speak, but couldn't.

"Don't die, Bear," I whispered. "In Jesus's name, we need you."

And Troth said, "In Nerthus's name, you must live."

But sometime in the night—neither Troth nor I knew exactly when—Bear did die. At dawn, when we found him so, we wept.

We had only our hands to dig his grave into the red earth. He never seemed smaller in body than he was then. As for the grave, it was far too shallow, but it was the best we could do.

I made the best Christian prayer I could.

Troth lay her sprig of hawthorn over his heart.

Then we covered him with earth.

As I sat by his grave, I refused to think of him as dead, tried not to think that I had lost my real father. Instead, I made myself see him in my thoughts as he was that time after we had fled with Troth, when Bear and I danced and played in that wretched little town.

How fine it was to see Bear perform again! I could hardly keep from grinning even as I played. In truth, never were Bear and I more together than when I piped and he danced. Here was this great and powerful man, a giant to most, his beard aflame, his fleshy face ripe with life, his small eyes as bright as any lofty star, gamboling as if he were some two-day kid sprung new upon a dewy world. How light he was upon his feet, his arms beating the air like angel wings aflutter!

Though no man was ever more earthbound than my Bear, none seemed to leap more heavenward. In truth, Bear's dance that time did not have the exuberance he had had before, and that lessening was sore poignant to my heart. But I had no doubt that God Himself, looking down, would not hold back His sweet smile at the sight of His cavorting, unchained Bear.

Oh, dear, great Bear in ragged tunic, whose soul fairly burst with the sheer joy of living, a breathing blessing to all who saw him, who bore a heart of loving grace, whose great hands would have gentled all the world if they but could—how I did adore him!

And since no mortal man can forgive sins, I took him as he was for all and all and ever would be.

Amen.

* * *

It was late of the morning, when Troth and I finally left Bear's grave—unmarked save for our tears.

We did not look back.

I do not know how long we wandered, save we went aimlessly about the countryside, avoiding all dwellings, people, and towns, finding food as we might. We did not speak to another soul and hardly to one another. Sometimes there was rain. Sometimes there was sun. Day and night rolled their endless wheel. It was all one to me.

It was Troth, in time, who said, "Crispin, we must decide where to go."

"Why?"

"We can't wander forever."

"Troth," I cried, "I don't know where to go."

Then she said, "Do you remember that place Bear spoke of, that land where there are no armies, no governments, no wars?"

"The land of ice?"

She nodded. "Perhaps we should go there."

"Troth, it may not even exist."

"Aude would say—that's why we should go."

Perhaps I had wandered enough. Perhaps I could no longer be weary. Something in what Troth said had stirred me. I heard myself speak: "I know what Bear would say to such a notion."

"What?"

"He'd laugh and then cry out, 'Crispin, if that place doesn't exist, we must make it so. Let it be as it *may* be!'"

And so it was that Troth and I, though weighted down by all that had happened, were guided by what Bear had told us: that freedom is not merely to be, but to choose. We chose to go to toward the edge of the world.

Wherever that might be.

AUTHOR'S NOTE

While the story of *Crispin: At the Edge of the World* is fictional, it is based on a number of historical facts.

Briefly, the end of the fourteenth century marked a time of great turmoil and change, moving England toward modernity. Recurring plagues and famines reduced the population by perhaps as much as half, bringing considerable social upheaval.

Four years after the time when this tale is set, the great peasant uprising of 1381 erupted. Led by the priest John Ball, among others, great numbers of peasants, and what we would call middle-class people, rose up in southern England and tried to end English feudalism, while establishing new personal and economic freedoms. (Whereas John Ball is an historical person, his brotherhood, as depicted in this story, is imagined.) With great bloodshed and destruction, the rebels almost succeeded in their goal of transforming English society, only to be suppressed by more bloodshed and destruction.

Edward III, the old English king, died in 1377, leaving the boy king, Richard II, on the throne. He would be overthrown while in his twenties.

At the time of this story, the Hundred Years' War was ongoing. This war—really a series of wars—began in 1337 and did not end until 1453—116 years later! Fought principally between England and France, it had to do with who should rule France, as well as with English claims—and French counter-claims—to large parts of what is today modern France. The war did not end until France, led by Joan of Arc, swept the English away.

In the course of this long period of hostilities, with its many great battles (Crécy, Agincourt) and truces, abandoned soldiers—free companies—would go on fighting for their own need and greed in much the way that Richard Dudley—a fictional character—does here.

The ancient English town of Rye still exists, though with changing coastal patterns it now sits inland. The burning of the town by French and Castilian forces took place in 1377.

The cog—the kind of ship that takes Bear, Crispin, and Troth to Brittany—was widely used during this time by Atlantic coast countries. Many relics of these ships have been uncovered. A complete reconstruction of such a ship, the Bremen Cog, as it is called, has been sailed. A good deal of information about the Bremen Cog may be found on the Internet.

Bastides, such as the fictionalized town of Bources depicted here, were fourteenth-century market towns and small cities built in the French Aquitaine. They were designed so that residents might defend themselves against French or English attacks or those deemed heretics by the Catholic Church. The town described here is closely modeled upon the real circular bastide, Fourcès.

Regarding the religion practiced by Aude: at the time of this story Christianity is absolutely the established religion of England. That said, all kinds of pagan beliefs and practices continued here and there. I refer readers to Kathleen Herbert's book, *Looking for the Lost Gods of England*. But one need only look at the origin of the English names for the days of the week and months to see the extraordinary persistence of old religions into even our own time. Indeed, Easter, the holiest day in the Christian calendar, derives its English name from a pagan Northumbrian goddess.

The best summary description of this fascinating period I know is the brilliant and captivating series of lectures delivered by Professor Teofilo F. Ruiz titled *Medieval Europe, Crisis and Renewal*, as recorded by The Teaching Company.